The Haunting of Kildoran Abbey

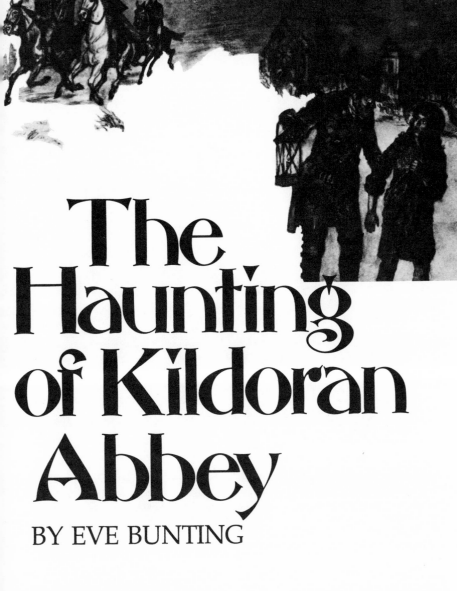

The Haunting of Kildoran Abbey

BY EVE BUNTING

FREDERICK WARNE

NEW YORK • LONDON

Frederick Warne & Co., Inc.
New York, New York

Manufactured in the United States of America
LCC: 77-84601
ISBN: 0-7232-6152-0

1 2 3 4 5 6 7 8 9 10

To the memory of my mother

I

THE WHISPER

The muffled sound of horses' hooves coming fast across the soft-packed snow wakened Columb to the knowledge of instant danger.

"Finn," he whispered urgently, "wake up!"

Finn slept on. One bony arm hid his face.

"Finn!" Columb threw off the ragged blanket and ran across the mud floor of the cottage to the other pallet. He shook his brother's shoulder. "Come on, Finn. Wake up, can't you! There's horses coming, and I think old Mick was right. I think it's the soldiers."

Finn was awake at once.

They ran to the door. Outside, the snow was falling again in big soft flakes. To the east, Slieve Donnard jutted out of the horizon like some humped white monster. At its foot, Lough Crae shimmered with ice, while to the west the thatch-roofed cottages of Ballykern were all but hidden in the swirling snow. The two boys shivered in their threadbare breeches and weskits.

"Poor Ireland," Finn said, looking up at the heavy gray sky with its promise of more snow to come. "Is it not enough to have famine and disease without having to suffer the worst winter in living memory? I tell you, Com, the year 1847 will go down in the history books!"

"Never mind poor Ireland right now," Columb said sharply. "It's us, the poor Mullen twins, I'm worrying about this day. Finn, can you see anything yet? There's a lot of them, there's no doubt about that, and they're coming along the bog road from Ballykern. But are they headed here?"

Finn pointed. "There. By the boreen. Jakers, Com! There's dozens of them."

"Dragoons," Columb said. "The First Royal Dragoons!" He shaded his eyes with his hand from the snow glare. "Quick, Finn, get the two gold pieces from the thatch. I'll put together what's left of the food."

Columb tipped the remains of the Indian corn into the ragged blanket from his bed. On top of the corn he put the cabbage leaves and the bunch of dried seaweed. Then he tied the four corners together in a knot and slung the bundle over his shoulder.

Finn came bursting in the door, the two gold pieces shining in his hand. "You keep them, Com. I have holes in my breeches."

Columb slipped the two coins in his pocket.

They sat down back to back on the dirt floor and pulled on their cracked and broken boots.

"The knife—did you remember the knife?" Finn asked.

Columb ran to the corner of the cottage, scraped back the loose mud of the floor and uncovered the hunting knife. He stuck it in his belt and pulled his weskit down to cover it.

Outside, horses coughed and stamped their feet.

"Dragoons, halt!" The voice was loud and full of authority. "Dragoons, dismount!"

Columb and Finn faced the entrance. Their legs were planted wide apart and their heads were high.

"Open up there!" A heavy fist struck the rough pine door, again and again.

"The door's open," Columb said in a steady voice.

The latch clicked and a sergeant walked in. He was warmly dressed in the thick blue uniform of a cavalry soldier, and he was so big that his head brushed the roof of the cottage. His face was red and shiny and his white mustaches brindled with frost. When he spoke, his voice hung in a warm mist on the dank air. "Boys, where is your father?"

Columb hesitated. "He is dead, sir, and our mother too. Famine fever it was. Both of them. We buried our mother a month ago." In spite of himself, his voice quivered.

Finn took over. "What do you want of us, sir?"

The sergeant slapped his gauntlets against his leg and frowned. "How old are you, boy?"

"We are both fifteen," Finn said. "My brother is the older by ten minutes."

"Twins you'll be, then," the sergeant said. "I can see that with my own eyes. Red hair and freckles and a bad look about the pair of you. Have you family? Uncles, aunts, someone you can go to?"

"We have an uncle in Boston, America," Finn said.

"And one in Ballykern," Columb added quickly, looking warningly at his brother.

"Good, good." The sergeant's smile left his eyes cold as ice. "I have orders to evict this family for nonpayment of rent. You're on Sir James Blunt's land, and he wants it cleared."

"Whether the rent's paid or not," Columb muttered.

"This cottage and the others on the holding are to come down today. We have our orders."

"We heard about it," Columb said quietly. "My brother and I are ready."

"Get along with you, then." The sergeant moved from the door. "We have work to do."

Columb swallowed. "Come on, Finn."

For the last time, they walked together out of the cottage that had been their home.

The soldiers shuffled their feet and rubbed their hands together to keep warm. Their eyes turned from the boys as they passed.

Columb saw two horses and riders behind the soldiers, standing apart from the rest. They were a man and a boy, richly dressed in plaid cloaks and woolen breeches. Their

9

boots were of soft, smooth leather. Columb recognized the man—Sir James Blunt himself, lord of the manor, the most hated man in all County Waterford. The boy was a stranger. Columb guessed him to be perhaps a few months older than himself.

As the boys drew level with the horse the boy was riding, the animal shied and the boy was thrown suddenly sideways on the saddle.

"You stupid oaf!" he yelled, lifting his riding crop.

Finn instinctively covered his head with his arm, but the crop never came down. Instead, as Finn looked up, Columb heard the boy whisper something. For a second he thought he had imagined it, for the boy was patting his horse's neck and saying aloud, "You're not worth dirtying my crop on!"

Then he saw Finn's face with its look of incredulity. He had not imagined it. The boy had whispered something, and Finn had heard.

When they reached the first rise on the road, they stopped to look back. The cottage was already just a small heap of rubble against the whiteness of the snow.

> *"I remember, I remember*
> *The house where I was born,*
> *The little window where the sun*
> *Came peeping in at morn."*

Finn's voice was a soft whisper, soft as the falling snow itself. "Do you mind the evenings before the hunger? Mother and Father, and the singing and laughing around the turf fire? The smell of potatoes or the stirabout cooking in the big black pot on the hob? And old Sweeney grunting in the corner? I swear, old Sweeney was the fattest, greediest pig in all County Waterford!"

Columb felt a lump in his throat at the memory. He looked over the bare desolation of the countryside. "Will Ireland ever recover from this, Finn? Will there be potatoes again for the digging and work for everybody, or has it all gone forever?"

"I tell you, Com, 1846 will be remembered forever, and it looks like 1847 will be no different." Finn spoke quietly, but there was a terrible conviction in his voice. "Someday the whole world will know what the English did to the Irish. I'm not blaming England for the potato blight, mind, nor yet for the sickness, but I'm blaming them for not caring and for not helping. They have more food over there than they know what to do with. But that English rascal Trevelyan who has charge of the British moneybags would rather use it to feed cattle than ship it to us. The Irish will remember, though. There'll be a time when England will be sorry, and it'll be too late. We'll not all be dead, Com, and the seeds of hatred have been sown."

The two boys stood in the falling snow, each busy with his own thoughts.

"Come on, Finn," Columb said at last. "We must keep moving if we're to get to our uncle's house before dark."

"What uncle?" Finn asked. "I wondered about that."

"You don't want to go to the workhouse, do you? If you don't have anybody, that's where they put you. We'll be all right, Finn. We have each other."

"That boy, the one on the horse, he said something to me. Or maybe he didn't. I think he said, 'Kildoran Abbey. Tonight.'"

"Kildoran Abbey! That's just a pile of old ruins; and besides, it's haunted." Columb's voice was thoughtful. "What did he mean?"

"I don't know. But there was something about the way he looked at me. I think we should go there. Besides, we can shelter in the abbey as well as anywhere else."

"But it's all of six miles on the other side of Ballykern." Columb lifted one foot and squinted at the old, worn boot. "That's a brave long walk."

"So?" Finn asked. "Have you something else to do the day? Or is it the ghosts you're afeard of?"

Columb grinned. "I was always afeard of ghosts, even though I know there's no such thing! Maybe we'll find

Obadiah before we get to the abbey. It would be the quare ghost that would tackle him!"

"Aye. And we'll go and see old Mick on our way through the village. It's been a wheen of weeks since we saw him last. Not since Mother died."

The thought of old Mick spurred them on, and they bent together against the swirling snow on the bog road to Ballykern.

2

WITCH

They reached the outskirts of Ballykern about noon. The snow had stopped falling, but the sky was still full of it. From Tor Head, a high cropping of rock that guarded the town, they could see the whole length of the village.

"It looks deserted," Columb said. "Where is everybody? There's nobody in the streets, even."

Finn pointed. "That's turf smoke coming out of old Mick's chimney. But most of the cottages have no fire at all. Did you ever know an Irishman to let his fire out? Something's wrong."

Columb opened their bundle of food. He took out the cabbage leaves and retied the corners of the rag.

"Eat, Finn! We'd best go down there with something in our bellies."

Finn brushed snow from the cold rock and sat down. He wiped sweat from his brow. "I mind when we could run to Tor Head and back of a morning," he said. "Look at me! My legs are weak as water."

"Aye, we ran, but we likely had a brave meal of porridge or spuds before we started." Columb chewed the cabbage hungrily. "We'll have a fire later, when we get to the abbey. We can make corn mash. The Yellow Peril doesn't taste so bad when it's hot. The dulse and the rest of the corn will do tomorrow."

The two boys fell silent. They didn't worry about the future. Sufficient food for today was remarkable. Sufficient for today and tomorrow was a miracle. And the day after tomorrow was a long way off.

Down below, the cottages of Ballykern huddled silently in the white valley, their brown thatched roofs, checkered with snow patches, the only color in the frozen landscape. Even the lazily winding river Suir gleamed whitely as it reflected the heavy trees. Ballykern had always been a busy market town, its streets lively with people. On fair days this was where the tenant farmers brought whatever grain and corn they had left after paying their rents. In the days before the famine, Main Street had been noisy with bargaining, the chatter of haggling, deals being made, "luck pennies" being exchanged. Today it was empty, lifeless.

"Something's moving on the river," Finn said suddenly. "Coming round the bend from Clonmel."

The two boys rose. A heavy barge was ploughing downstream. It was escorted on either bank by two of the Queen's mounted cavalry. On its stern a blue-coated soldier leaned against a great gray bulk.

"It's a cannon," Columb said.

As they watched, they saw the soldier swivel the cannon so that it swept silently across the left-hand river bank, then the right.

"Jakers," Columb breathed. "What in the name of Kathleen ni Houlihan have they got in there?"

"There's nothing left in the whole of Holy Ireland that's that valuable," Finn said. "It's heading for Waterford town, likely. For the exporting. Now what's going out of the country in times like these? The only thing we've got plenty of is starving people, and that nobody wants, least of all England. Could it be—?" His voice trailed off, for Columb was no longer beside him. He swung around just in time to see his brother fling himself in a flying tackle at a small figure, running like a rat across the snow. Under the rat's arm was their precious bundle of food.

"Got you, you thieving spalpeen!" There was grim satisfaction in Columb's voice as he rolled on top of the boy, his arms right around the thin body.

Finn ran over. As Columb released his grip, Finn grabbed the boy by the neck of his tattered jersey and hauled him off the ground so that he hung dangling at Finn's mercy. His feet in their wet, moldering boots were a good six inches off the ground.

"Let go of me, you big Yahoo. I'll put the Curse of Cromwell on the two of you if you don't take your dirty big hands off of me!"

Finn laughed. "You're spunky for such a wee one. What's your name, young fellow?"

"Butter and cream," the boy answered. "What's yours?" Beneath his dirty brown duncher cap green eyes flashed impudently.

Finn shook him gently, still grinning. "Don't give me any back chat. I asked for your name."

The boy stuck out his tongue and kicked Finn on the shins. It was a well-placed kick.

"You gulpin!" Finn shook the boy like a barley stook on threshing day.

The tweed cap slipped sideways and toppled off into the snow. Long, black hair, freed from its covering, tumbled crazily in a tangled mass.

Columb broke the silence. "Jakers," he said, "he's a girl!"

Finn lowered the girl quickly to the ground. She walked to her cap, picked it up, knocked the snow off and placed it back on her head. Angrily she crammed all the black mass of hair beneath it again.

"I'm not a girl," she said flatly. "If you want to know, I'm a witch, and I wasn't codding when I said I'd put the Curse of Cromwell on you. I can do it, never fear." She glared at one boy, then the other. "Big galoots!"

Columb and Finn shuffled uneasily under her stare.

"Well, what were you stealing for?" Columb asked sheepishly. "You shouldn't have stolen our food."

"I stole it because I was hungry," the girl said. "I was blue mouldy for the want of food, if you must know."

"We'd have given you some if you'd asked," Finn said.

"Huh!" The grunt expressed her disbelief.

"Here." Columb untied the bundle and offered it to her.

She glanced at him once, quickly, and then took a piece of the dulse, the black iodine-tasting seaweed that was now scarce as diamonds in the seas around hungry Ireland. She tore at the dulse ravenously. Her teeth were small and white and pointed. Her eyes, Columb noticed, were a pale, pale shade of green.

"Have another piece," he said. "We have enough."

She chewed in silence as the boys watched her.

"My name is Ryan O'Callahan," she said at last, "but you can call me Witch."

"Go on with you," Columb said. "You're no more witch than I am. Witches are old and ugly, and you're no more than fifteen and I've seen worse-looking."

"Begob and I'm a witch," the girl said, "and I'll prove it to you." She turned her strange green eyes from Columb to Finn. "*You* know I'm a witch," she said.

Columb saw Finn shiver.

"You're a twin," she said slowly.

Columb hooted with laughter. "Oh, faith and you're a witch all right. Only a witch would know a thing like that, and us the spitting image of each other."

Finn said nothing.

"You're a twin and an orphan," she went on, her face turned toward Finn. Her voice had a strange, high, singing tone. "You're a dreamer of dreams and a speaker of words. You are a follower, not a leader. The two of you have a love of Holy Ireland that's greater than even you know, but you'll find out the bigness of that love one day, with the sacrifice, and that day is coming soon. Heed me, for I know."

The boys were silent.

Her eyes turned to Columb. "You are a doer. And Ireland has a need of the doers to balance her dreamers. Your name, and that of your brother, will be known in your whole townland, aye, and in the whole of the province. Irishmen will bless it and Englishmen will curse it."

The whole world seemed to be hushed and listening. Witch's eyes lolled upward, and her breathing quickened, then quieted. When she spoke, her voice was normal again. "What do they call you?" she asked.

"If you're a witch you don't need the telling," Columb said.

"I don't be bothered with little things like names," Witch said haughtily. "I only worry about the future."

"I'm Columb Mullen, and he's Finn. We're on our way to Kildoran Abbey."

"I'm with you," Witch said, rising briskly. "I feel like a new woman after that dulse, and it's plain as a pikestaff you two need looking after. Some spalpeen might happen by and steal the rest of your food when you're not looking! But what's at the abbey, besides haunts, I mean?"

"We don't know," Columb said. "First, we're going to Ballykern to see old Mick, and then we'll look for Obadiah."

"Who's Obadiah?" Witch raised her hand as Columb made to speak. "I know. If I'm a true witch I wouldn't need to ask. But I don't concern myself with people, just the future. I swear," she added sadly, "nobody has the understanding of witches at all at all."

"Obadiah isn't people. He's our dog. At least, he was our dog. We had to turn him out to fend for himself a while back, when the hunger got so bad. We hear tell he's turned wild now, but he'll remember us. He has a lair for himself in the low bog on the far side of town. Finn knows where he'll be. We used to go there to hunt, before the hunger."

"Is he still alive, do you think?" Witch asked. "I haven't seen hide nor hair of a dog in all the county this twelvemonth."

"He's alive all right." Finn grinned. "Old Mick's seen him a wheen of times. 'A big streak of a shadow,' Mick called him.

He's a hunter, that dog! He'll have found some way to stay alive."

"He's smarter than most then," Witch said.

The three looked at each other. Gaunt, hollow-cheeked, ragged—and they were three of the lucky ones.

"By the holy Paul!" Columb heard the shake of anger in his own voice. "There'll soon be as few Irish left alive in Ireland as there are Indians in America! But there's a day of reckoning coming, and maybe we three'll be a part of it."

Finn put his hand on his brother's shoulder. "Come on then, Com, let's go. It'll be all right, so."

As they walked down the hill to Ballykern, Columb thought about what Witch had said. "You have a greater love for Holy Ireland than even you know." She was part right and part wrong, he thought. He had the love, but he knew the strength of it. Whatever the sacrifice that he was to be called to make, if it was in the name of Ireland, he would make it gladly. He heard Finn ask, "Tell us the future then, Witch. What's waiting for us at Kildoran Abbey?"

"I only tell the far future," Witch answered crossly. "I've told you that already. What's waiting in Ballykern's likely bad enough."

Columb felt a surge of despair. It seemed suddenly as though they were the only ones left in the world. Then he remembered the barge and the soldiers and he asked, "Witch, did you see the barge on the river?"

"Aye, I saw it. Something in there the English don't want the Irish to have at any price."

"Look!" Finn pointed at the sky. "Look at that, would you, it's a good omen."

With the sudden change that's a part of Irish weather, the clouds had opened and a faint pang of sunshine shafted through the darkness. A tremble of rainbow looped the sky.

> ". . . add another hue
> Unto the rainbow, or with taper light
> To seek the beauteous eye of heaven to garnish,
> Is wasteful and ridiculous excess."

Finn's eyes were dreaming on the clear colors in the sky.

"What's that Gom talking about?" Witch asked, her voice for the first time unsure, hesitant.

Columb grinned. "It's probably William Shakespeare, Finn's favorite Englishman. Remember what you said? He's a speaker of words all right, my brother Finn!"

Witch shook her head in amazement.

"Look," Columb said. "The rainbow's arched clear across Ballykern, and it looks like it ends right at Kildoran Abbey. Maybe that's what we'll find there, a pot of gold! If the ghosts haven't found it first."

"I'd rather find a pot of food," Witch grumbled.

The boys laughed. In a sudden spurt of energy they all three linked arms and ran down the hill, through the shimmering pinks and greens and golds, all the way to Ballykern.

3

VILLAGE OF DEATH

The main street of Ballykern was called Tamany Road. It ran parallel to the river, curving where the river curved in a carelessly graceful sweep. The first cottage that faced the footpath belonged to the Brennan family—Patrick Brennan, his wife Rose, their four young daughters and three sons. Columb could never remember passing the house when the half-door wasn't open. Fat Mrs. Rose loved to lean across the bottom half, her red arms comfortably folded, smiling and talking to the passersby. Now the door was tightly closed. No smoke came from the chimney. Old Mick Cushenen's cottage was closed, too, but a faint wisp of blue turf smoke drifted lazily above the thick thatch of his roof.

Finn knocked with his knuckles on Mick's door while Columb and Witch stood a pace behind him. "Mick!" he shouted. "Let us in, Mick. It's me, and Com."

There was no sound from the cottage. No answering shout of welcome, no stamp of feet in heavy boots crossing the dirt floor.

"Mick!" he called again, stepping back. "I don't like this at all at all." He went to the small high-set window, brushed the thick snow from the sill, and peered in. "Mick's there," he said at last. "He's lying on his bed like a dead man." He looked at Columb and then at Witch.

In their minds was the same thought.

"The fever, is it?" Witch asked, her face paling.

"I don't know. But there's no use us all going in, just in case. I'll go."

"Why you?" Columb asked. "You stay with Witch. I'll go."

"Mick's more my friend than yours," Finn said quietly, and Columb nodded. He knew that was true. There had always been a deep and close tie between old Mick and quiet Finn. Many's the time, before the hunger, their mother had allowed Finn to stay the night in old Mick's cottage. Mick loved to talk, and Finn to listen, and it had been from him that Finn had learned all the tales of ancient Ireland; the stories of Brian Boru and Garret Mor, of Hugh O'Neill and the victory at Yellow Ford. Mick had been a "hedge teacher," teaching Irish children to read and write the Gaelic anywhere a group gathered and was ready to listen. It was he who had fired Finn's imagination with his stories of the great patriots— Daniel O'Connell and Thomas Davis, leader of "Young Ireland." And Finn, in turn, had inspired Columb.

"It won't be long now, Finn, till you're old enough to join 'Young Ireland,' " Mick had said. "Aaragh, I envy you, boy. Your generation will drive the English out of our country once and for all!"

Old Mick hated the English with a deep and steady abomination. He had fought in the insurrection of '98 and had been one of the Wexford Boys, captured at Vinegar Hill. His contempt for the English was the mainstay of his life, and he watched their every move with baleful eyes. "That Lord John Russell is going to be worse than Peel, Finn. I'd rather have a

Tory than a Whig any day of the week. He'll knuckle down to Trevelyan and it'll be fair field and no favor against poor Ireland. We'll die by the hundreds, aye by the thousands, and we'll look for help to our lord and master, almighty England, and then God save us all. She'll watch us die and be glad to be rid of us. We're nothing but a thorn in the flesh to the English lion, and that's all we've ever been."

Finn had listened and believed, and as time passed, he had seen it all happen as Mick had said. When their parents had died, Mick had wanted the boys to live with him in Bally-kern, but they had refused. They would stay in their own home as long as they could. Afterward they would fend for themselves, for the life they had led had taught them the value of independence.

Finn had learned something else from old Mick. He had learned about books and poetry.

"The only good thing the English ever birthed were their writers," old Mick had explained. "Now, wouldn't you wonder how the likes of them could produce Shakespeare and Milton and Dryden? Och, sure there must have been some Irish blood in those fellows somewhere, to be able to speak the words that way. They're the only English words I've ever heard worth listening to!"

Now, as Finn broke the glass in the small window and squeezed through, he knew a quick fear that Mick, too, was dead. He crossed to the old four-poster bed with the brass knobs on each corner where he had slept so many nights, curled at Mick's back. Mick had held on to the bed when everything else except his precious books had been sold to buy food. "Mine will likely be the only bed left in Ballykern," Mick had said wryly, "but I was born in it, and by the holy Paul, I'll die in it too."

The old man lay still and peaceful. His great gray beard spilled luxuriantly over the ragged brown blanket.

"Mick!" Finn put his hand on Mick's shoulder and shook it gently. "Mick," he said again.

The blue-veined eyelids fluttered.

Finn touched Mick's forehead and then his thin hands. They were dry and cool. "Com! Witch!" he called. "There's no fever. He's awful weak, though. It's starvation."

He pulled the heavy bolt and opened the door.

Columb was already untying their food bundle as he came in, glancing anxiously at old Mick's waxen face.

Finn hurried to stack more of the dry, crumbly bits of turf in the big hearth. They caught fire immediately with a whish of bright orange sparks.

"Och, the poor ould fellow," Witch said pityingly. "I'll make corn gruel. If it's watery enough we'll get some down him!" She half filled the hanging black pot with water from the bucket by the hearth and stirred in two handfuls of yellow corn.

"He's not long in his bed," Columb said, "no more than a day, for the ashes in the hearth pit were still alive and that water's near fresh from the well."

Finn knelt by his old friend's bed while Witch stirred the pot.

Books were stacked everywhere—on the floor, in battered boxes beside the bed, against the chimney wall.

Columb peered on shelves and inside the corner cupboard. "Not a smithering of food in the place." His hand brushed some dry stuff on a high shelf and he pulled it down. "Begob and he was eating grass," he whispered.

They looked at the still figure in the bed.

"We should have come to Mick sooner," Columb said. "He's only an old man when you come to think about it. Too old to fend for himself."

"I thought he was indestructible." Finn's voice was so low they could scarcely hear him. "I thought we would be the burden to him."

"Likely makes no difference." Witch blew the steam from the pot away from her face. "I'm thinking there's no food anyplace within miles of Ballykern."

"Sir James Blunt has food, at the manor," Columb said.

"Aye, but he'll not be parting with any of it." Witch

spooned some of the gruel from the pot and tested it with the tip of her tongue. Columb heard her stomach growl with hunger.

"Finn, I'm going into Brennan's," he said. "Maybe they've left the place, but I have to see."

The opening and closing of the door let in a coldness that was like death itself.

"Don't die, Mick," Finn whispered fiercely. "You're too tough and too mean to die."

"Here!" Witch was beside him with a tin plate in her hands. "Get out of my road," she said, pushing Finn to one side. "With those ham hands of yours you'd likely choke him." She raised the old man's head and held the spoon gently to his lips.

"Come on, ould fellow. Get this good warm stuff inside you. It'll do you a power of good, so it will. Witch made it for you. It's a witch's brew, full of spells and charms. It's me own recipe." Her voice was a soft croon, sweet as a lullaby.

The gruel dripped from the corners of the old man's lips and trickled down his chin.

Patiently Witch trapped it in the wooden spoon and fed it back to him.

"It's no use." Finn's hand pulled nervously at a corner of the blanket. "We're too late."

Witch turned on him angrily. "Faith and I hate people who give up at the first go off. Go on in with Columb. You're as much use here as a banty cock in a henhouse."

Finn stumbled outside into the white silence.

Columb was leaning against Brennan's door, holding his stomach. "What'll we do, Finn?" he asked. His voice was choked. "They're all starving in there, every last one of them. They can't talk, even. Oh, Finn!" He closed his eyes and shuddered. "Remember Mrs. Rose? You wouldn't know her for the same person. They're all skeletons. Their poor bones are breaking through the skin. If we can't get food into them they're finished." He rubbed his hand across his face. "Does Witch have enough gruel made to feed them all?"

Finn nodded. His eyes were frightened. "Com, how many people would you say live in Ballykern?"

"A hundred," Columb said, "or maybe even a wheen more."

"And we have enough corn and dulse for maybe twenty?"

"Aye, if we make the gruel thin enough. But if there's food to be bought we have the two gold pieces."

"The 'going-to-America' gold pieces," Finn said.

They looked at each other, sick at heart. Their father! Columb remembered their father! Sevenpence a day he had been paid for the work on the roads, and he had walked six miles to and from the digging, in sleet and rain, to make it. It had taken five months of backbreaking labor to save the sovereigns. "We'll not be going, your mother and me," he had said, showing his sons where he had hidden the money in the thatch. "We'll live and die here, in our own country, but you'll go. There's nothing here for the young anymore, but despair. Go to your Uncle Eamonn in Boston. I never thought I'd live to see the day I told my sons to leave Ireland, but it's the only hope left for the two of you." Columb remembered how Finn had drawn a rough map of America on the dirt outside the cottage door. Their father had marked Boston with an "x." One day, that would be their home.

Now they stood, silently remembering.

Com spoke first. "We just can't walk away from this, Finn. These are our people. We have to get food and get it fast, for I'm thinking every soul in Ballykern is dying this day."

"Aye. Dying or close to it," Finn said. He pushed open old Mick's door.

Witch greeted them triumphantly. "Would you look at this now? The ould fellow's swallowing!" She placed the spoon at Mick's lips.

Slowly his mouth opened. The muscles on his thin cheeks twitched feebly and the gruel trickled down his throat.

"I've got nearly the whole of the bowlful into him," Witch said, "and dael the haet lost."

Columb allowed them a few seconds of joy. "Witch," he

said, "there are six people next door. You'll have to feed them. Finn and I are going to find food."

Witch pushed the long black hair away from her face. She laughed briefly. "You're going to find food! And do you think if there was food for the finding that the whole of Ballykern would be starving?"

"We have two gold pieces," Finn said shortly. "There may be some to buy."

Witch pursed her lips in a silent whistle. "Begob and it's a pair of gentry I've fallen in with. Money and everything! Are you planning on feeding the whole town?"

"Come on, Finn," Columb said. "Witch, leave Mick now and see if you can help the Brennans. We're going to the manor."

"Good luck to you." Witch poured a stream of thin yellow gruel into the bowl and blew on it to cool it. "Sir James is not likely to give you anything for the peasants, no, nor sell it either."

For a second, Columb's hand touched the handle of the hunting knife. "First he'll have the chance to sell it," he said grimly. "Let him refuse and he'll be the sorry man."

Before they left, they carried in a glowing turf and kindled a fire in Brennan's hearth. The warmth and light in the gloom of the cottage promised life and hope. Witch was already coaxing gruel into the youngest of the children. Then they walked silently up Tamany Road through the shadows of early evening that settled on the trees and darkened the slow-flowing river. The rainbow had gone with the sun.

They met no one on the road. Two thick spirals of blue smoke rose straight and strong into the sky from the Brennan and Cushenen cottages. Behind the dark and shuttered doors they passed lay the dead and dying, without hope, like withered leaves left by the wind.

"Begob and I hope Sir James enjoyed his dinner the day," Columb said angrily. "Bad cess to him! If we don't get what we want, he may never enjoy another one." In his pocket he touched the cool gold of the coins. With his other hand he gripped the thonged leather handle of the hunting knife so tightly that he felt it bruise his palm. The heat of anger in his heart was good, for he knew if the anger went, all he would have left would be despair. He thought about Sir James Blunt, and he nursed his anger to keep it hot so that he would be ready.

4

BLUNT MANOR

Blunt Manor was about a mile outside the village. A broad driveway swept importantly from the road to the front of the house. It had been freshly cleared of snow and the sharp gravel stones hurt Columb's feet through the thin soles of his boots.

"It's a grand house his Lordship has, to be sure," he said softly, "with a grand view of the devastation."

On all sides of the big gray granite manor white fields rolled to meet the distant white hills. Through the snow poked the black, blighted tops of the diseased potato plants. Underneath, the praties themselves rotted in the putrefying earth. Even muffled by the clean snow the stench was over-powering.

Finn wrinkled his nose in disgust.

"Faith and if I were himself with all of his money, I'd take myself off to one of my other fancy houses till the smell died down."

"What," Columb answered, "and miss the great chance to take over all the tenant farms when the people are in trouble? You're not thinking like his Lordship."

They climbed the three wide steps that led to the black oaken door. Columb pulled the rope that hung from the lintel. A bell clanged, deep inside the house, echoing and reechoing into a fading silence.

The door opened. A tall thin footman in wine-colored livery looked at them suspiciously. "Yes?"

"We've come to see Sir James," Columb said. "It's important."

"Sir James is not at home."

The door was about to slam when Columb's foot stopped it, holding it open. "He's home, and we mean to see him. We have money. The people of Ballykern are starving and we want to ask him, civilly, to sell us food."

"Get out of here before I throw you out on your ear. Sir James is not home to you or the likes of you."

His voice infuriated Columb. It was an Irish voice, overlaid with a thin coating of fake English. One of our own who sold out for a full belly and warm feet, he thought contemptuously, and all at once his hands were on the footman's throat and he was shaking him in mindless fury, pushing him back through the door into the entrance hall.

"Stop it, Columb! It's not that Paddy we want. Save your strength." Finn tugged at Columb's arm. "Come on, leave him be."

The footman cowered against the wall and rubbed the red marks on his neck. The faint croaking noise he made was enough. Through a swinging green door four men came on the run. One wore the same wine-colored livery. The other three were dressed in rough gamekeepers' clothing.

In a second, Columb and Finn were surrounded. Back to back, they faced the four.

"How are you doing, Finn, you solid man?" Columb asked gleefully, bunching his fists. "It's a while since we had a good fight."

"What's going on here?" The voice was young and arrogant and unmistakably English. On the curve of the wide staircase stood the boy who had been on horseback with Sir James that morning.

"It's these two boys, Master Christopher. They're after forcing their way in here. They were asking for Sir James."

"Well, then, they must see Sir James." The boy yawned

behind his hand. "You don't think they'll cause trouble, do you? Those two?" There was contempt in the eyes that swept over Columb and Finn, from their shaggy red hair to their shabby wet boots.

One of the men laughed, but the tall thin footman spoke up angrily. "Making to choke me, that one was." He pointed to Finn and then to Columb in confusion. "He's dangerous, so he is."

"Really?" The boy raised an eyebrow. "I would have thought you could have handled an underfed, dirty, common person like that with no trouble, Murphy—a man of your physique."

One of the men tittered again, and Murphy stood back muttering to himself.

"Now the thick talks like the rest of us," Columb said, with a laugh. "His grand accent's gone entirely."

The boy, Christopher, came down the three remaining stairs and crossed the polished slab floor to Columb and Finn. "I am Christopher Piddington. I am living here for the present with Sir James. What is your business with him?" The boy's face was arrogant, his voice bored.

Columb and Finn exchanged a quick glance and Columb knew Finn was thinking what he was thinking. This boy would not possibly have any dealings with them. Finn must have imagined the whispered words this morning. He spoke loudly.

"Our business is with Sir James. We tell it to nobody save him."

The boy laughed briefly. "This way then, my good fellows. I'll take you to Sir James." He turned back up the staircase, and Finn and Columb followed him.

Christopher moved silently in his black velvet slippers. The boys' boots echoed noisily on the polished wood. Christopher rapped on a door at the head of the staircase and threw it open. "Two young gentlemen to see you, Sir James. I think you met them already, briefly, this morning." He stood aside for the boys to enter.

Sir James sat in a massive chair by a roaring fire, a glass of wine in his hand. The room was his bedchamber, and it was immense. Thick velvet draperies were drawn against the early evening chill. He was wearing a rich dark green dressing gown and matching slippers, the gold cord of the robe stretched taut against the soft roundness of his belly. A ruby glass decanter of wine and a plate of cheese were on a small table beside the chair. The thick, cloying sick-sweet smell of rotting potatoes outside mingled with the inside air.

Finn stepped ahead of Columb and spoke. "God save you, Sir, and all in this house. We have come, respectfully, to tell you of the condition of your people in Ballykern. They are starving, Sir, and near to death. My brother and I have gold. We know of nowhere else to buy food and so we ask you, Sir, to sell us some."

Sir James watched him unblinking.

The boy, Christopher, leaned against the door, smiling in amusement.

Columb stared straight ahead, his hands by his side.

Sir James cut a portion of cheese and ate it slowly. He spoke with his mouth full. "Who are you, boy?"

"I am Finn Mullen. My brother, Columb."

"Mullen? Mullen?" Sir James chewed thoughtfully. "Ah, yes. Your father didn't pay all of his last year's rent."

"My father is dead, Sir," Finn said quietly. "He paid you what he could."

"This money—this gold you have, let me see it."

Columb took the two sovereigns from his pocket and placed them beside the wine decanter on the table. They gleamed red in the firelight.

"I'm indebted to you, boy," Sir James said. He picked up the gold pieces and balanced them in his hand. "Honesty is always to be commended, and it's a heartwarming thing when a father has sons to fulfill his obligations." He poured a stream of ruby wine into his glass and drank deeply. "Christopher, show the young gentlemen out."

Two long strides carried Columb behind Sir James's chair! The hunting knife glittered evilly in his hand. "Don't move, my fine master," he said softly. With one hand he pulled Sir James back by his long hair. His other hand held the point of the knife to the man's throat. The boy, Christopher, still leaned against the door and it seemed to Columb that he still smiled.

"Oh, Sir James!" Christopher's voice trembled and the smile was gone as though it had never been. "That ruffian is going to kill you. Don't move, I pray you, dear Sir James. What is it you two boys want?" His knees shook in his velvet breeches.

"We want food." Finn crossed the floor to stand by his brother's side. "And we want plenty of it. We're not thieves." He nodded toward the two gold pieces. "We'll pay for it."

"All right, all right," Christopher said. "Just don't hurt Sir James. Oh, Sir James, my poor gentleman, why did I ever allow these villains into your presence?"

Sir James sat motionless, his eyes on the big freckled hand so steady on the knife.

"Give them what they want," he whispered. There was no fear in his voice. There was acceptance and cold anger.

"You!" Columb said to Christopher. "Take my brother to your storage rooms. We'll need saddlebags. Four will be enough. Fill them with grain, corn, flour, anything you can find. Order two horses for us. When you come back here, I'll release Sir James."

"I'll hurry, Sir James," Christopher said eagerly. "Pray stay still. I fear for your life."

Columb's hand moved slightly and the knife point pricked the skin. "His life is not worth more than another man's."

Sir James's eyes glittered yellow in the firelight.

Finn opened the door. "Lead the way," he said to Christopher, "and hurry." As Christopher closed the door behind them he added, "I have a place to go tonight." He looked closely at Christopher as he spoke.

Christopher laughed quietly.

"That you have," he said. "I wasn't wrong. You two are what we want at Kildoran Abbey."

"You seem to have recovered quickly from your terrible fright."

"Ah, my cowardice comes and goes," Christopher said. "I find it a useful flaw in my character."

The two men who stood guard at the bottom of the stairs touched their hands to their foreheads in respect as Christopher passed.

"We're to have six saddlebags to the larder," Christopher said. "Sir James's orders. And three horses, saddled, to the front door. This way," he said to Finn.

The larder was a room twice as big as the bedchamber upstairs. Its cold stone floors and walls made it perfect for storage.

At the sight of the food, Finn gasped. Great hams and cheeses hung from hooks on the ceiling. Earthen crocks held milk and butter. Lined along the walls, bulging sacks spilled grain and oats and wheat. Loaves of soda bread, wheaten farls, and currant bannocks cooled on wooden tables. Finn swallowed.

"Here!" Christopher thrust a wheaten scone and a hunk of smooth yellow cheese into Finn's hands. "Eat while we wait."

Finn's legs crumpled and he sat heavily on the cold stone floor.

Christopher watched as Finn crammed the food into his mouth. There was terrible pity on his face. "There's more food at the abbey," he said gently. "You can have more there. We'll—" He stopped, listening to the footsteps outside the door.

"Here you are, Master Christopher. Six saddlebags. The horses will be to the front in a few minutes." The servant's voice was a mixture of servility and curiosity.

"Thank you," Christopher said. "You can go now."

Together they filled two of the bags with flour, one with

wheat, and one with grain. A whole side of ham went into another, and the last one held four round cheeses.

"Right," said Christopher. "Now we have someone put these on the horses, go back and get your brother, and you take me, unwillingly of course, as your hostage. That way you'll get clear away. You're saving me a lot of work, you know. Ballykern was next on our list."

"Whose list, of what?" Finn tightened the last buckle on the saddlebag.

"The boyos' list," Christopher said with a grin. "We've no time now. You'll learn all about it later." He opened the door. "Murphy! O'Hare! Bowers! Come and get these saddlebags. They're to be strapped on the horses." They climbed the stairs again.

"I can feel my cowardice returning," Christopher whispered. "It always comes on suddenly."

The knife still glittered, a point of light, at Sir James's throat. "All set?" Columb asked.

Finn nodded.

"Good man." He let go of Sir James's hair, managing to give it a last tug of farewell. "You're lucky," he whispered. "If Finn hadn't come back—sswish!" He made a sweeping motion with the knife across his own throat and grinned.

Sir James rubbed his throat and watched Columb with narrowed eyes. "I'll not forget you, Columb Mullen. We'll meet again."

"We'd best take this young gentleman with us, for security," Finn said, nodding toward Christopher.

"Oh no, no, please don't take me. You'll hurt me. Sir James, don't let them take me."

"Try not to snivel," Sir James said coldly. "They'll not harm you."

Columb looked at Christopher in disgust. "Faith and you're a right brave Englishman," he said. "Come on, Finn. Let's go. We're wasting time." The knife was back in his pocket, his hand on the handle. "Don't be tempted to touch that bell rope till we're long gone, Sir James." He nodded toward Christopher. "I don't like the English, and one less wouldn't bother me any."

Christopher wrung his hands. "Do whatever they ask, Sir James," he whispered. "I don't want to be killed. My father would be very angry if you got me killed."

Columb pulled him roughly by the arm. "So don't follow us, your Lordship, and we'll return him by morning, and the horses, too. Come after us, and he's dead."

They ran quickly down the wide staircase, Christopher in front. The four servants watched them sullenly from the hallway, but no one made to stop them.

"Is everything all right, Master Christopher?" Murphy asked.

Christopher nodded. "I'll be back shortly. Sir James does not wish to be disturbed." He took a warm wrap from the hall rack.

Columb looked at him sharply. What sort of game was the English boy playing?

The horses moved restlessly outside the door.

"Hoi! Giddy-up!" They were in the saddles and away.

"Yahoo!" Columb shouted into the still night air. His long red hair, windspun, whipped out behind him. "Begob and we did it, Finn!" he yelled over his shoulder. "Aren't we the quare pair of boyos?"

"You are and all. I'll testify to that." The English boy's Irish brogue was fake and strange.

Columb felt a quick resentment. Let him speak his own language. What call had he to make fun of theirs?

They reined their horses to a halt in a steaming, warm-breathing circle.

"Who and what are you, anyway?" Columb leaned across the neck of his horse to peer closely at Christopher.

"I'm a friend. A friend to Ireland and a friend to you too, if you'll have me."

The horses scratched at the hard snow and whinnied, impatient to be off. In the fast-gathering dark, horses and riders were only faceless blurs against the sky and the trees and the slow-moving river.

Christopher stretched out a hand to Columb.

Columb shook his head. "I don't shake the hand of an Englishman. Never did and never will."

Before Christopher's hand could fall to his side, Finn wheeled his horse, leaned across and took it. "I'll shake with you," he said. "On faith. Maybe Com's right. But I think Ireland needs all the friends she can get these days, and that goes for the Mullens too."

"Come on," Columb said sharply. "We've got work to do." He dug his heels into the horse's side and set his head toward Ballykern.

The heavy saddlebags bulged and swayed against the sides of the nervous horses. They rode quietly, the steam of their breathing mingling with the steam of the horses' breath.

There was another creature abroad that night. A creature who smelled the food and who followed them like a shadow, waiting for his chance. He had not eaten in three days, but he knew he would eat tonight, even if it meant a killing. He made no sound, and the distance between him and the horses lessened with every second. Saliva dripped steadily from his great jaws, leaving a dark trail on the white snow.

5

THE HAUNTED ABBEY

At the beginning of Tamany Road they pulled their horses to a skidding halt. In the slow-falling dark, Ballykern looked more than ever like a town deserted. The lonely street lined by the silent cottages was strange as a dream.

Finn shivered.

> *"No sun—no moon!*
> *No morn—no noon!*
> *No dawn—no dusk—no proper time of day."*

He stroked his horse's head. "It's enough to scare you. The ghosts of Kildoran Abbey could move in here anytime."

Bright orange sparks suddenly shot into the sky at the other end of the village.

"Mick's fire!"

"Aye." Columb smiled. "Witch is likely making a few spells over the hot turfs."

"Who's Witch?" Christopher asked. He was behind the other two, struggling with his horse. The animal was frightened. He shied nervously, pawing the ground with his forefeet. "Steady, boy!" Christopher said, patting his neck. "What in the dickens is the matter with you? There's nothing to be afraid of."

The horse moved sideways again, snorting, his head rolling in panic.

Christopher dismounted, keeping a tight grip on the reins. His feet in their thin velvet slippers slithered on the glassy road surface. "Come on now," he murmured, "you'll—"

Finn and Columb saw the danger first.

"Look out, Christopher!" Finn yelled.

A great dark shape hurled itself out of the shadows and clawed the side of the frightened horse.

The horse whinnied in terror and tried to run.

Christopher, stunned by the suddenness of the attack, planted his feet apart and hauled on the reins.

The horse's legs spread-eagled and he went down with a heavy thud, screaming in fear.

The other animal lunged again, on top of the horse, knocking Christopher from his feet. He fell across the horse's head, the reins tangled around his arms and body.

Columb and Finn were off their horses in the same instant.

"Take the reins, Finn!" Columb shouted, thrusting the

bridle from his animal into Finn's hands. "We'll lose them all if we don't mind."

The noise was ferocious. All the horses were snorting and screaming. Finn struggled to hold his two, his words of reassurance lost in the uproar around them. Columb disentangled Christopher and hauled him up.

"Great heavens," Christopher panted, "what is it?"

The huge, gaunt beast was worrying the leather saddlebag, growling deep in his throat.

"He smells the ham," Columb said. "The brute's starving, like the rest of us." He pulled his hunting knife from his pocket, crouched low and moved forward. Poised to spring, one arm raised, he hesitated. "Holy suffering saints!" he whispered. "It's Obadiah."

At the sound of the name the big beast stiffened and the growling ceased.

"Obadiah!" Finn called. "Obadiah!"

The shaggy orange head turned. The golden eyes gleamed through the darkness.

"Come here, Obadiah," Columb said gently. "Here, boy! Stay still," he whispered to Christopher under his breath.

The horse on the ground, sensing a change of mood in his attacker, tried to rise and screamed as his legs slipped away beneath him.

Obadiah stood motionless, teeth bared. His head lifted, listening, smelling. Then he moved. In two bounds he reached Columb, tail wagging, his great tongue lolling in delight.

"Obadiah, you ould blether!" Columb rubbed the big dog's head and laughed aloud in relief. "Faith and I'm glad you remember us. You had me worried there for a minute!"

Obadiah directed his attention to Finn. He leapt up, front paws on Finn's shoulders, slavering all over Finn's face.

"You big galoot!" Finn tried to hold the horses with one hand and fend off the dog with the other. "Your breath smells like Pat Hogue's midden!"

"Help me here, Columb." Christopher was taking off his cloak. He lifted the horse's legs and spread the cloak on the ground beneath them. "Pull on his head, Columb. He should be able to get a grip with his hooves now."

Christopher got behind the horse and heaved while Columb pulled on the reins. In a few seconds the horse was up and, by the way he moved, all right.

"Nothing broken," Columb said, feeling along the animal's legs and the sides of his ribs.

Christopher opened the saddlebag that had been underneath when the horse fell. "Flattened flour," he said, grinning. He shook the wet from his cloak and slung it again around his shoulders.

Columb did not return his grin. Instead he bent to pat Obadiah. "Come on, ould fellow, follow us. You'll have to wait to eat, like the rest of us."

They mounted their horses again and galloped off, the big dog loping behind them.

It was fully dark now. There was an arrow of moon in the sky, but it was not high enough to shed its light. No friendly lamps gleamed from the cottage windows.

"We'd best hurry," Finn said. "I'm only hoping we're not too late!"

They looped their horses' reins around a boulder in front of Mick's cottage and unbuckled the saddlebags. Witch's face appeared at the broken window, and then she was at the door.

"How's Mick?" Finn asked. "And the Brennans?"

"Doing rightly. Did you get the food?" She squinted through the darkness at Christopher. "Who's he when he's at home?"

Before Finn could answer, Obadiah edged into the patch of light from the open door.

"Bless us this day!" Witch stared at Obadiah with a mixture of fear and astonishment. "Is it all the strays of the world you do be bringing home with you?"

"Mind who you're calling a stray," Finn said. "That there's

a fine specimen of Irish wolfhound. That's Obadiah. Remember? We told you about him. And this is Christopher Piddington. He helped us get the food."

Witch moved aside to let them in, eyeing the dog and Christopher with equal suspicion.

Christopher grinned and swept off his cloak.

The dog slunk sheepishly to the fire, lay down, and began to lick the ice from his paws.

The boys slung the saddlebags on the table and opened them.

"Well, I'll be jakered," Witch muttered, closing her eyes ecstatically. "Did you ever see the likes of that?"

In the pale circle of light from the hurricane lamp the saddlebags spilled their rich harvest. They looked at it in reverent silence.

"There's no time to waste," Christopher said. "Sir James may decide to take the chance and follow us anyway. Let's divide the food and give it out."

Witch raised her eyebrows. "Faith and it's English, and it's giving its orders like the little gentleman it is!"

Finn grinned. "Save your breath to cool your porridge, Witch. He's all right. It's only good sense he's talking. We'll explain all about him later."

Columb grunted. "You can explain him to me then, when you're at it."

Finn crossed the kitchen to Mick's bed. The old man's faded blue eyes were open, and a smile quivered the edges of his beard.

"Good man, Mick." Finn laid his hand for a second against the sunken cheek. "It 'ud take more than a good starving to finish you off!"

"Come on, Finn," Columb called. "We've got work to do."

Witch was slicing the cheeses into sections while Christopher cut the ham. Obadiah drooled at their feet.

"I'd like to give you some, dog," Christopher said, "but there's people to be fed, and they come first."

Witch gave a piece of cheese to Columb and a piece to Finn.

Columb wolfed his in two bites, his thin throat swallowing convulsively. Finn shook his head. "I had some," he said. "Save it for the others."

Witch tossed the hard rinds to Obadiah. "That'll hold you for a wheen of minutes," she said. "Witch'll get you something later, never fear."

Columb repacked the sliced ham and cheeses in the saddlebags. "Finn, get some bowls. The people are too weak to come to us. We'll have to go to them. Witch, leave food and water for Mick where he can reach it himself. Then you come too."

As they left the cottage, Witch picked up a tin pan and a big spoon. "My gong," she said with a grin.

They buckled the saddlebags back on the horses and started up the road on foot, leading the animals, the big hound pacing at their sides.

Witch banged with the spoon on the pan. "Open up your doors, everybody," she yelled. "We have food for all who can stomach it. Open your doors and see what the boyos have for you."

The pale yellow moon climbed the sky, silver-shadowing the silent street. A few doors creaked open, painfully, slowly.

"Come on, everybody. You can open up. You've heard tell of the Boys from Wexford? Well, these are the Boys from Waterford! They went to see Sir James, and out of the goodness of his heart, God bless him, he sent food for one and all."

Lamps were being lit and held high in open doorways. Their wan gleam showed bony arms, hollow faces, shaking bodies.

"Here, Mrs. Slattery! Flour for you and a bowl of wheat. Ham for your pan and oats enough for a week's stirabout." Finn and Columb and Christopher were working at top speed, dealing out the food. Witch kept up a constant flow of chatter.

"Those that can walk, take for those that can't. Break down the doors if you have to, but feed the sick ones tonight. Ballykern's not finished yet."

Women sobbed and cried with joy. Pinafores and shawls bulged with their burden of grain. Bowls were held out in trembling hands. Thin children hugged their arms about their scrawny bodies and stared silently at the food.

"God's blessing on you, boyos, and on you too, young mistress."

"May all the saints look down on you this night." The faces turned to the boys were desperate for hope.

"I'm thinking we're none too soon, Finn," Columb muttered grimly. "There's more doors closed than open." He took Witch's pan and spoon and leapt up on the stone wall that ringed the village well. The six saddlebags were empty. He banged for silence.

"Listen, everybody," he said. "We bought this food from Sir James. He didn't want to sell it, but we bought it anyway. We would have stolen it if we had to. No matter. Bought or stolen, he'll be mad as a boar by now. Hide whatever you don't eat tonight for they may come looking for it, and for us, too. Say nothing. You have enough for a week, and I'm promising you something this night. There'll be more when that's done. I don't know where it'll come from, but you'll not starve. I promise you this, me, Columb Mullen. See that all in Ballykern eat this night."

As he jumped down, a few faint cheers came from the people. An old woman in a tattered black shawl stepped forward.

"I knew your father, Columb Mullen," she said. "He was as fine a man as ever drew breath. I'm thinking this night he would be proud of his sons." She touched Columb's hand briefly. Then her arm moved in a circle that gathered in Witch and the three boyos. "Ballykern thanks you. We'll not be forgetting."

"Come on, Witch." Columb's voice was husky. He jumped on his horse and pulled Witch up in front of him. "Let's go."

Christopher and Finn were already mounted. With the soft pad of hooves on snow they galloped out of the village and into the night.

Columb felt the people watching them till they were out of sight around the bend of road and river. He imagined them then, moving back to their cottages, starting up fires, cooking food to feed themselves and their neighbors. Ballykern was saved for now, and he had made the promise. Somehow he knew he would keep it.

The rush of dark wind blew Witch's hair in tangles across Columb's face. Ahead of them he could hear the creak of harness and the muffled squish of the other horses. The dark shadow moving beside them was Obadiah.

"Are you ready for the ghosts now?" Columb whispered, his mouth against Witch's ear.

"Aye. They couldn't look any worse than the ones in Ballykern. What are we going there for anyway? Have you found out?"

"Finn thinks we should; that's all I know. He's mighty taken with his English friend."

"You're right," Witch said. "I've been noticing that. An Irishman taking an Englishman to friend. Begob it's as hard to believe as a blue-eyed bullock! Do you think we can trust him, this fine English gentleman?"

Columb laughed. The sound seemed to hang on the thin night air. "I wouldn't trust an Englishman if the Holy Pope of Rome himself vouched for him."

Witch was silent. When she spoke, her voice had the strange, high, keening note that Columb had heard before when she foretold their future. Her body was rigid and suddenly cold against his.

"I see a prison, with bars on the windows and locks on the doors. I see Finn Mullen inside. And there are others there, too. A tall one and a small one—and me—I'm there too. And we can't get out, we can't get out and— Oh, help us, somebody help us!" Her voice sank to a whisper. "But there's nobody to help us, for we're all our lone and there's nobody that cares."

They rode in silence. When she spoke again, her voice was

normal. "We must be nearly there. I don't hear the other horses."

Columb's arm tightened about her. "Witch, you just made another prophecy. Do you remember?"

Witch shook her head. "I never remember afterwards. It all leaves my head, like it had never been."

Columb frowned. She had said she saw Finn Mullen and others, but not a word about Com Mullen. Where was he? What had happened to him?

Ahead of them, the black bulk of the abbey suddenly showed itself against the surrounding darkness. Moonlight lay pale on crumbling stone walls, a moss-covered tower with a rusted bell, a fragile buttress with a broken crucifix silhouetted against the night sky. Finn and Christopher were nowhere in sight.

"Well, where are the ghosts, then? I don't—" Witch began.

All at once their horse shied sideways and snorted. On the ground, Obadiah growled deep in his throat, his hackles rising like stiff orange-colored brushes.

"Jaymedy Mike! What's that?" Witch's voice was small and quavering in the darkness.

Columb gripped her arm. "Sh!"

From the abbey came a high-pitched, terrifying scream. It rose to a wild mad shriek, like the cry of a banshee, shivered against the ancient stones and was lost in the whiteness of the night. That was no human sound.

Columb felt his scalp prickle.

Witch turned her back to the abbey and buried her face against Columb's chest. "Oh, Com, I'm afraid. It's the ghosts, Com. Let's turn now before it's too late. The ghosts don't want us here."

Columb shook his head. He nudged his horse with his heels and urged him slowly forward into the moonless shadows of the waiting abbey.

41

6

THE UNDERGROUND ROOM

The night silence was unnatural. Now that the screeching had ceased, it was as though the whole countryside waited, trembling, listening. The soft clop-clop of their horse, Witch's shallow breathing, the stealthy pad of the dog's feet, even the pounding of his own heart, seemed loud in the hush around them.

"Columb!" Christopher's voice shattered the silence. "I didn't tell you what to expect here at the abbey. You and Finn and I seem to have been together for so long. I forget you hadn't been here before." He peered up at them. "That noise you heard. That was one of us—our sentry, to be precise. We found a sort of funnel up in the bell tower and if you scream into it, it changes the sound somehow and makes great ghost noises. It keeps snoopers away from the abbey. They think it's haunted anyway. What they don't know is that the haunting of Kildoran Abbey is done by a bunch of boyos, not a clutch of ghosts!"

Beside him, Finn grinned wickedly, enjoying their surprise.

The remembrance of her fear added an extra sharpness to Witch's tongue. "You big Yahoo. It's a crack on the ear you're needing, scaring us like that! Forgot to tell us indeed. Och, but what else could we expect from an Englishman?" She turned her face from him. "Sure you can't make a silk purse out of a sow's ear, nor a decent man from an Englishman."

"Aaragh now, Witch, don't be so mad," Finn said. "Sure we were just stepping back to warn you what to expect when the screeching started."

Columb slid from his horse and helped Witch off.

"All right now," he told Christopher, "take us wherever we're going and tell us what this is all about. We've had enough mystery for one night."

"Tie your horse over there with ours," Christopher said. "They'll be out of sight in case anyone should be brave enough to come this close. Then follow me."

There was even less light behind the tumbled walls than on the moonlit countryside. Christopher led the way. Shadows shifted and re-formed on the rubble-strewn ground. The crunching sound of their footsteps on the patches of frozen snow, the rattle of dislodged pebbles beneath their boots, echoed eerily in the cold silence.

Witch walked close to Columb. "I'm scared as a sheep at shearing time," she whispered. "Are you meaning to tell me we're going to spend the night in this place? All night?" She shivered and grabbed his arm. "Keep a good hold on that knife of yours, Com. They say cold steel can't cut a ghost, but it gives me a better feeling anyways."

Christopher led them along a crumbling stone path that had once been cloisters leading from church to refectory. The east wall of the refectory still stood, its once-sacred stones derelict and forgotten.

"Watch it, right there!" Christopher stopped and pointed to where the path had caved in, leaving a deep, jagged hole. It was partly overgrown with snow-thick weeds so that it was almost completely concealed. They skirted it cautiously.

"Here we are." Christopher moved to the jagged wall at the north end of the refectory. What had once been a fireplace was still visible, the huge hearth and chimney opening choked with nettles and long grasses. He scooped an armful of wet weeds aside to reveal a smooth slab of stone and fumbled with something at the side of the hearth. There was a rusty, creaking movement and then, slowly, heavily, the slab slid back.

Columb could see narrow, winding steps leading downward into blackness.

"I'll go first," Christopher said, stepping inside. "Be careful, though. The steps are uneven and some of them are broken. Hold on to each other, and guide yourselves with one hand on the wall."

When they were all through the opening he reached up and pulled an iron ring set high on the roof. Slowly, the slab moved across again, leaving them in complete darkness. The air was dank and icy cold.

"Are you all right, Witch?" Columb's voice was ghostly in the darkness.

Witch gulped. "It's like a tomb up in Glasnevin, so it is."

"Count the steps," Christopher said. "There are twenty. When you get to the bottom there's a short passageway."

They moved slowly downward.

"Eighteen, nineteen, twenty." Witch counted under her breath. "Thanks be to Saint Brigid we've got this length." The passageway was narrow and smelled of earth. Cobwebs brushed their faces and once something small and furry darted across Columb's foot. He felt everyone stop and heard Christopher's voice.

"Open up. It's me, Christopher."

Muffled sounds came from somewhere in front and then a voice, thick with a Waterford brogue, asked, "And what's the password, if you please?"

"Young Ireland."

"Right you are," the voice said cheerfully. "Hold your whist then till I get this thing opened."

There was a rumble of a heavy bolt being pulled and then the creak of a door opening. Light came into the passageway, and a warmth of air, and the mouth-watering smell of meat cooking.

A boy stood in the doorway, a hurricane lamp in his hand. He was tall and thin, with a mane of white hair, and his eyes glowed red in the lamplight. His smile was warm as cream.

Christopher stepped past him and beckoned the others inside.

Columb looked around in amazement. They were in a large room with an earthen floor and gray stone walls. There was a fireplace in one corner. A black pot swung from its iron bar over the blazing turfs. Scattered around the room were a half dozen high-backed wooden chairs. Against one wall a long, black trestle table held dishes and food.

There were two other boys in the room, apart from the one who had opened the door. They sat at the table and watched Columb and Finn and Witch and Obadiah closely.

"Is everything all right?" Christopher asked.

The white-haired boy answered, and Columb noticed that his eyes were not red, as he had first thought, but a strange, pale shade of pink. "As right as rain," he said. "Tinker's still up in the tower on guard. We heard him wailing at you a while back. Some fellow came by early in the day, nosing about, and Tinker had to scare him off." He grinned widely. "Tinker says he ran like a billy goat and likely hasn't stopped yet."

"This is Witch," Christopher said. "And these two are Finn and Columb Mullen. If you want to know which is which, Finn is the one who'll talk to me, Columb is the one who won't! The dog is Obadiah. They all need food, but Obadiah doesn't look like he's going to wait!"

The big dog had leapt across the room to the table and was standing with his two front paws on the top of it. His jowls ran juices as he slobbered over the small morsels left on the plates.

"Hold on there, fellow. You'll be fed." The boy at the table put down a length of rope that he had been twisting and winding and got to his feet. He was small and wiry with a cowlick that stood up like a cockscomb at the back of his head. His eyebrows met across his eyes in a black scowl. All of his movements were swift and deft and capable. He scraped some leavings from the dishes onto a tin plate and put it on the floor for Obadiah.

"By the holy Paul!" Witch spoke incredulously. "It must be a great thing to have that much food in front of you in these sad times that you can afford to leave the half of it on your plates. What kind of a quare place is this, anyways?"

"Oh, we always have enough food here. Nobody goes

hungry. Sir James is the generous provider, though he doesn't know it. I bring some every time I come to the abbey." Christopher took his cloak off and hung it across a chair. "Rat, will you bring plates over here and get us some stew out of the pot? Sit down, and we'll eat," he told the others.

Finn and Columb and Witch sat at the table with the other two boys.

"This is Roper O'Neill." Christopher nodded to the dark-haired boy with the cowlick. The boy had picked up his rope again and was working with it intently. "And this little one here is Skibbereen."

The other boy at the table looked at them shyly and smiled. He was maybe five years old, with big round brown eyes and black hair that curled over his head in small ringlets. He didn't speak.

The pink-eyed boy brought steaming plates from the black pot on the fire.

"This is Rat Reilly," Christopher said, lifting his spoon.

"Don't you mind being called Rat?" Witch asked hesitantly.

The boy smiled his warm smile and shrugged his shoulders. "Och, I've gotten used to it. What's true's true after all, and I suppose I do look like a rat. The real name for what I am is an albino, but sure nobody knows that, or cares either. So Rat I am, and Rat I'll stay. Besides, it goes so well with Reilly that I can't complain."

Columb could see that Witch had stopped listening. The smell of the stew wafted across the table, and he knew that her whole being was aching, longing for the food, just as his was.

"Jakers," she muttered. "If there's vittles like this, I'm staying, and I'll fight any ghost that tries to put me out!" Her spoon clattered against her plate.

Obadiah was pushing his tin dish around and around on the floor, licking off the last scent of flavor.

Christopher spoke with his mouth full. "Roper over here is a very useful man to have with us. He can do anything in the world with a rope — almost make it sit up and beg. When we raided the granary at Crossgarvin it was Roper got the grain out. He threw his rope up over the weathercock, skinned up the walls, and threw the sacks down to us as he filled them. Easy as anything, wasn't it, Roper?"

Roper scowled. He played with his rope without lifting his head. "Aye, that wasn't bad. But roping the chickens out of his Lordship's henhouse wasn't so easy, especially since you wanted it done with no squawking."

The little black-haired boy turned his eyes from one to the other as they talked, listening intently.

"What do they call you?" Witch asked him. She looked wistfully at her empty plate.

"Skibbereen," the little boy whispered.

"Skibbereen. Why, that's a grand name altogether." She picked up the plate and looked at it. "Would it be all right to lick this? Some of the gravy's going to waste."

The little boy nodded.

"And what age are you, Skibbereen?"

"Skibbereen," the boy whispered again.

"Ay, I heard that," Witch said, licking her plate for all she was worth. "But I want to know what age you are."

"Skibbereen," the boy whispered.

"Witch, you've got a blob of grease on your nose." Columb pointed with his spoon.

"Have I now? Well, it won't do to lose it!" Witch curled her tongue up as far as it would go. She licked her lips. "Begob and that was the best stew I ever tasted in all my born days. You'll excuse me for gobbling it down like a cormorant, but I was powerful hungry." She settled back contentedly in her chair. "Now then, what was that you were telling me? Your name's Skibbereen, you're Skibbereen years old. I suppose if I ask you the time of day you'll tell me Skibbereen!"

"Skibbereen," the boy whispered. "Skibbereen."

Christopher had been watching and listening in silence. "Rat found him one night, out on the bog. He was almost dead. That was two or three weeks ago and he hasn't said a single word but 'Skibbereen' since."

"Skibbereen's a town in the west of County Cork," Finn said. "I heard tell they had the hunger there worse than anywhere in all Ireland, and the fever too. I heard tell that every soul in that town died from the one or the other. They say the sights in Skibbereen would have put you mad for the looking."

"Skibbereen." The little boy's eyes filled with tears. They trickled silently down his cheeks and onto the table.

Witch pushed her chair back and knelt beside him. "There, there," she murmured. "Hush now, Acushla. You're not to be thinking about bad things. You're here now, you're safe. Witch'll love you. You'll be Witch's little boy." She wiped his eyes with the palm of her hand and rocked his head against her chest.

He snuffled loudly. "Skibbereen," he whispered. "Skibbereen."

There was a banging on the heavy wooden door. "It's me, Tinker," someone shouted. "Let me in."

"What's the password, then?" Rat asked.

"Give over with that nonsense. Who do you think we are? The Black Hand? You know it's me, so open the door."

"It's Tinker," Rat said with a grin. He pulled back the iron bar and opened the door.

"Well," Witch muttered. "Bless us and take care of us and keep us out of the road of carts! What a plaster!" A dirty red spotted handkerchief was tied around the new boy's long, greasy hair. His nose was as beaked as a fighting cock's, and from one ear hung a single golden hoop.

"Is it a woman you'll be, or a man?" Witch asked, eyeing him up and down.

With a fierce growl Obadiah launched himself through the air. He hit the boy in the doorway, knocking him off his feet. The boy fell with a thud, half in, half out. Obadiah stood growling, his massive paws on the boy's chest, his teeth inches from his throat.

"Obadiah!" Finn shouted. "Get back here, you spalpeen!"

Out of nowhere a knife appeared in the boy's hand and his

arm curved back to strike, but Columb was suddenly behind him, gripping his wrist. The knife fell with a clatter to the floor.

"Easy, now, easy," Columb said softly. "Don't kill the dog. Obadiah, get off of there."

Still growling faintly, Obadiah drew back. His eyes glinted yellow in the lamplight.

Finn held him around the neck, whispering to him, rubbing between his ears.

The boy rose, shrugging off Columb's hand as he tried to help him.

"Leave me be," he said. "I would have killed that big baste, so I would, if you'd let me." He turned angry eyes to Christopher. "Where did the dog come from? And the rest of them?"

"They're friends," Christopher said. "Columb and Finn and Witch." He shrugged. "And this is Tinker."

"I'm sorry about the dog." Finn held out his hand. "I don't know what got into him. He's always been good around people. He was all right with the others."

Tinker curled his lips. He shook Finn's hand reluctantly. "I hate dogs. Everywhere we made camp they came, whining and barking and stealing our food. And they hate me. They can smell it off me, the hate. You can always smell hate." He picked his knife up off the floor and wiped it on his trousers. Then suddenly he threw it. It curved in a wide arc and stuck, quivering in the dirt, half an inch from the dog's paw.

Obadiah yelped and leapt backward.

Tinker laughed. "Next time it'll be your gizzard, you mangy craiter!"

Columb slowly pulled the knife out of the floor and balanced it in his hand. "Is that so?" He flicked his wrist. Effortlessly the knife glided through the air and landed, shuddering, a scant hairbreadth from Tinker's foot.

Nobody spoke. Then Christopher said, "I was just about to remark that Tinker's our knife man. Seems we have two. That will be useful, as long as we remember that our enemies are outside the abbey, not amongst ourselves."

"Aye, and they're not Irish; they're English," Witch said. "Present company excepted of course." She smiled sweetly at Christopher.

Tinker and Columb eyed each other across the room. Then Tinker bent, pulled his knife from the dirt, spat on its blade, and drew its edge across his fingers.

Columb watched him.

Witch belched, breaking the silence. She pointed her finger at Christopher. "What I'd like to find out is what's an Englishman doing helping the Irish get food. For as sure as gun's iron I never heard tell of the likes of that before."

Christopher stacked some dry turfs on the fire and nudged them with the toe of the slipper. "Pull your chairs over here," he said. "If you want to know, I'll tell you."

"What about another sentry in the tower?" Finn asked.

"We don't need one this late. Nobody comes here, especially not after dark."

"Aye," Rat said. "And it gets awful cold up in that bell tower at night. Besides, there's the hole in the path for a bear trap if anyone came."

"What about the smoke from the fire?" Witch asked. "Would somebody not see that?"

"We don't light it in the daylight. At night it would never be noticed. The church is taller than the refectory and hides us from Ballykern."

"All right, Christopher, tell us everything." Witch settled herself comfortably. "If we're to be here together we have to be able to trust each other and it doesn't come easy, you know, you being what you are."

Columb grunted.

"Com," Witch said, "your face is as long as a Lurgan spade. Give the fellow a chance to speak."

In the circle of light from the fire they waited for him to begin.

7

FOOTSTEPS IN THE NIGHT

"I come from Dolby in the County of Somerset. You know my name is Piddington. Well, my father is Roger Laverne Piddington, Earl of Castleton. He is a very rich man and very powerful, but he's fair and just. I believe he is a good man. I have no mother. She died when I was very young, and I am an only child."

"Tch, tch," Witch murmured. "Your mother dying and you with no brothers to call your own. You supped your sorrow with a long spoon, so you did. I had six brothers myself, you know, but they're all gone, all in America."

"When my father had to go to India on business for Her Majesty, we planned that I should go too," Christopher said.

"There's a lot of Irish in the army there," Finn's voice was vague. "Mick told me. Doing England's dirty work as usual."

"My father thought it best that I shouldn't face the long journey. Sir James Blunt has a home in Somerset built on land that he leases from my father. He was coming over here to Waterford, to Blunt Manor, for a time, and it was decided that I should come with him. Over here, I could learn another side of the business of owning land and of tenant farming. For that's what I'll be someday. A landlord, like Sir James, but, I assure you, very unlike Sir James."

Witch sniffed. "I should hope you'd be different from that crabbit ould sepulchre! Just thinking about him would give a body the green gawks!"

Christopher smiled and went on. "The plan has been a big success. I've learned a lot. I've learned about starvation and desperation and power and cruelty. In fact, I've learned to be ashamed—of my country, my way of life, the indifference of people who should do something and don't." He stood motionless in front of the fire.

Nobody spoke. Witch had taken Skibbereen on the chair

beside her and she absently smoothed his black curls, twining them around her fingers. The dog twitched and groaned, dreaming perhaps of long-ago rabbits that ran, plump and free for the catching, on green Irish fields.

"I wrote to my father," Christopher continued, "but it takes a long time to get a letter to India. I expect he'll be back in England before I get an answer. I told him what it's like here. I told him about Sir James and of how he treats his tenants." Christopher slapped his fist into the palm of his other hand in frustration. "At first I tried to reason with Sir James. I made the mistake, you see, of thinking he was like other people. I tried to make him understand that his tenants were dying all around him and that he could save at least some of them. He wasn't interested. He thought me a fool to worry when I was well fed and comfortable."

A turf crumbled and slid in the hearth. Its red glow flickered for an instant across Christopher's angry face.

"Then I wrote to several friends of my father's asking for help. The letters I got back were unbelievable. Some of them enclosed clippings from English papers. The truth of it is, the English people don't understand or accept that things are as bad here as they really are. They think there's food, yes, and work and money to be earned. But they believe the Irish are just too shiftless and lazy to do anything but sit on their backsides and whine and cry for help." He paused and looked around the circle of hard young faces.

Tinker spat viciously into the fire, and there was a sudden hiss and sizzle.

"Do you see?" Christopher said, and his voice was pleading. "It's not that they're wicked, the ordinary people; they just don't understand. There's not a man I know in England who wouldn't give to someone in need, but they're angry. They think the Irish are begging because they'd rather beg than work. Columb? Do you see? You're wrong about the English, you know, no matter how you feel. We're not all bad. I grant you that you don't see the best of us in Ireland, but maybe, if we can get through this, we can change it—together."

Columb clasped his big hands in front of him and stared into the fire. He made Christopher no answer.

"The men I wrote to, they think I'm just a boy and don't know what I'm talking about. I could have gone home, I suppose, and I wanted to, for some of the things I saw here turned my stomach. The servants are still in our house, and I would have been all right. Sir James would probably have let me go if I had made it difficult enough for him. But the more I thought about it, the more I realized that if he wouldn't do anything, maybe I could. I hear talk around his table. I know where there's food to be had, easy, for the stealing. That cart of turnips, Rat. I knew that was going to be coming along the Mullintrae Road, for I heard Sir James tell O'Hare he was expecting it."

Rat nodded his head, his strange pink eyes staring at Christopher unblinkingly. "They were gey good turnips and plenty of them."

"And the same with the barrels of meal that we took out of Drogatown. Nobody suspects me. They think I'm a spineless fool, for that's what I've been careful to have them think. I needed others to help me, for there's things I can't do alone. The next thing I've planned I figured would take five. Now I've got five."

Witch looked around the group. "By my figuring, you've got seven and a dog."

"I'm not counting the girl, the dog, or Skibbereen. I need big, strong boyos for what I have in mind."

Witch bristled. "I'm as good or better nor any boyo any day. You could go a lot further and fare a lot worse."

"We'll have you put the hex on Sir James," Columb said soothingly. "That'll be your part in the destruction."

Finn stood and held out his hand to Christopher. "I'm thinking all here's beholden to you. Grand is no name for what you're doing. It's marvelous entirely."

Columb kept his seat. I wonder, he thought. All these years of hating and distrusting anything English. Maybe I'll just bide my time before I shake his hand. He yawned widely. "I mind my father used to tell me the English could spin a right good story if they had a mind to it." He stretched his arms over his head and yawned again.

"Och, give over, Com," Finn said. "Your old fiddle can only play one tune and we're all tired listening to it. I don't like the English either and well you know it, but a whole nation can't be bad. Give the fellow a chance."

Witch interrupted the tense silence. "How did you find this place at all at all?"

"Rat's the one who found it." Christopher's face was flushed and his voice was without its usual confidence. "Rat was the first boyo to work with me."

"Aye," Rat said. "I found it when I was just a wean. I used to come here to play in the abbey, for I was never afeared of the ghosts. I fell one day against the old fireplace outside and you could have used my eyeballs for marlie marbles I was that surprised! I used to come all the time after that. When my father and mother died and Sir James tumbled our cottage, I came here to live. It was nice. Better than the workhouse. Christopher spoke to me one day out on the boreen, and a wheen of days later I brought him here. We've been using it ever since."

Witch looked at him with admiration. "You mean to say you stayed here all on your ownio, in the middle of all the ghosts?"

"The ghosts don't bother me." Rat smiled his warm, quick smile. "There's good ghosts and bad ghosts, and the monks that lived here were kindly men. They'll not be harming us."

Witch leaned forward in her chair. "Did you ever see any of them, Rat Reilly?"

"No, I've never seen them, for there's nothing to see. But I've heard them. They're gentle as doves. Sure and they do only be coming back to their old holy places to pray and to sing their sacred songs. It was comforting of a night to hear them. I didn't feel so lonely, like."

"Aaragh!" Witch's eyes were cat green. "Are you codding me now or do you mean it?"

"I'm not codding. Wait a while and you'll hear them for yourself."

"What about you, Tinker?" Finn asked. "How do you come to be here?"

"Rat found me too, near dead of starvation, lying behind a hedge in Harry O'Donnell's field. I was trying to catch O'Donnell's old cow to see if there was any milk left in her. My ma and my da and my sister Kate were all famishing, back in our caravan. I couldn't get any farther than the hedge. Rat brought me here and fed me, but when we got back to the caravan they were all dead."

"Ochone, ochone," Witch murmured. "Sure my own died too. It's a sad thing to eat the dirt of loneliness."

"I've been eating dirt of some sort or another all my life," Tinker said. When he snarled, his lips drew back so that they met the beak of his nose. "My da mended pots and pans. We'd stop in a field or by the roadside and there was aye somebody to move us on, yelling and thumping with their sticks. Dirty thieving tinkers, they called us. Then like as not, they'd set the dogs on us. The very ones I'm helping you feed now wouldn't have fed us even when they had plenty."

"Och sure now, there's none of us has our sorrows to seek," Witch said, "and it's a bad thing to be warming up old grievances. What about you, Roper?"

"There's nothing to tell about me." Roper kept his eyes on his rope. "I have nobody now and I never had. But it's as well that way. One day I just walked out of the workhouse and never went back. They can look after somebody else in there. I can look after myself."

Skibbereen climbed down from Witch's chair and stroked Obadiah. Under his hand the big dog stirred and his tail quivered with pleasure. It was warm in the room, and they were full and comfortable. Roper swung his rope back and forth and it made a dull swishing sound in the quiet of the room.

"So what's this job you're planning?" Columb asked.

Instead of answering his question, Christopher asked another. "Have you heard of Henry John Johnson?"

Columb shook his head but Finn nodded. "He's a Quaker minister, isn't he? I mind old Mick talking about him. He and his friends are going the length and breadth of Ireland, feeding the hungry. Their church is called 'The Society of Friends.' They're terrible good people."

"Yes, they are. They're setting up soup kitchens in the worst-hit famine areas. They move as fast as they can, but that's not fast enough. They don't have much money, you see, for it all comes from contributions. What we've been doing is trying to steal enough food here in Waterford to keep the people alive till Johnson gets this length. We've done our best. We got the grain and the cartload of turnips. The chickens Roper stole made enough soup for the whole of Toberone. Tonight, Ballykern got fed. What we're really doing is buying time, for each hour a man lives is closer to the time when he'll get fed regularly. If Johnson can keep the people going through this winter and spring there'll be a new potato crop in the summer, and maybe, just maybe, it'll be a healthy one and the famine will be over." He thumped his hands on the arms of his chair. "But we've got to find food enough till Johnson gets here."

"When do you think that'll be?" Finn asked.

"It's the beginning of March now. He should be in Waterford by the end of the month. It'll be getting warmer then too, and so perhaps with a little food and the cold out of their bones the people will survive. Now, my plan is this. We've been stealing small. Now we're going to steal big. Enough in one swoop to feed the whole townland — Ballykern, Trellagh, Magheragh—enough to keep them going till the end of the month."

"Wait a minute now," Finn said. "I like the sounds of it all.

But one thing. Stealing's a vexing word to me. How can you steal something when it's yours by right? Any food that's in this poor miserable land belongs to the Irish. It's the English that stole it from us. So when we're only giving it back to the people that owns it, we should call it by a name other than stealing."

"Aye." Witch nodded. "Stealing's an ugly word, so it is." She belched gently again behind one hand. "What are you grinning at, Com, you big galoot?"

"Nothing at all at all," Columb said. "I was just minding the first time we, er, met. I know well you don't hold with stealing."

Witch turned her head from him, her face pious. "There's no good in stealing. We could call it maybe bargaining. It's near enough the same thing."

"Aye." Tinker shined his knife on his breeches, then turned it so it caught and reflected the fire flame. "And it'll be the truth. If they don't bargain with us we'll gut them like herrings. Food for their miserable lives. A good exchange, I'd say."

"What about this plan now?" Finn asked. "The one that's going to—"

"Whist!" Rat put his finger to his lips and cocked his head on one side. "There's somebody coming along the path from the abbey. He's in the cloisters."

Christopher raised the globe of the hurricane lamp and blew out the flame. In the shadows from the dying fire they stood together, listening. Obadiah growled, a low rumble, deep in his throat and Finn dropped to his knees beside him, one hand across his muzzle. Skibbereen, thumb in mouth, slept on, his curly head resting on the dog's back.

"My blood's froze like icicles on a wet thatch," Witch groaned. "Is it the ghosts, Rat? I'm afeard of ghosts."

Rat shook his head. "Ghosts don't wear boots."

The last turf slithered in the hearth and crumbled to white ashes. The room glowed briefly and darkened. Around them the old abbey creaked with its night life. And the steady thump of boots came closer and closer, echoing the quickened heartbeats of those in the underground room.

8

THE FIRST PRISONER

The silence was broken by a muffled yell and a dull thump. Then again there was silence.

"What is it?" Columb whispered.

"Whatever it is, it's fallen down the hole," Rat said.

Christopher felt his way toward the door. "I'll have to go and see what happened. The man could be hurt. Roper, you come with me. You may have to lower me down there. The rest of you stay here and be as quiet as you can. Don't light the lamp yet, for he might not be alone."

Rat slid back the bar on the door and as softly bolted it behind them again. "Nothing to do but wait," he whispered.

"I'd trade my old boots for a good cup of tea." Witch's grip on Columb's arm was blood-stopping tight.

"Sh!"

There was the faint creak of the stone slab as it slid across, then silence.

It seemed a long time to Columb before he heard the slab slide open again. There was the slow sound of feet in the passageway and then Christopher's voice. "Young Ireland."

Rat swung the door open.

"Light the lamp," Christopher said. "The boyos have just taken their first prisoner."

In the yellow lamplight Columb saw that Roper and the English boy carried an unconscious man between them. He bent forward to look closer. "Why, it's the fellow from the manor. The one that tries to sound like an Englishman though he was born and bred on the bogs!"

"Aye, it's Murphy." Roper let go of the man's legs. "When I

saw who it was I wanted to throw him back in the hole."

Murphy groaned and lifted one arm to shield his eyes from the light. "Where am I?" His voice was weak.

"Never mind that," Christopher said sharply.

Murphy swallowed and tried to raise his head. "Somebody hit me a powerful crack."

"Nobody hit you. You fell down a hole, and you would have been there yet if we hadn't pulled you out. Why did you come here?"

Murphy looked around, blinking, staring. Tinker, particularly, seemed to fascinate him. He kept his eyes riveted on him as he spoke. "It was Sir James. He offered a reward to whoever found Master Christopher and those two redheaded ones. He's terrible mad, so he is. One time before, I followed you, Master Christopher. I saw you climbing down the ivy from your bedchamber one night. You were supposed to be asleep, but you took out your horse and came here to the abbey. I lost you somewhere when you got this length."

Witch brought a tin cup of water and put it into his hand. Before he could raise it to his lips, Tinker sprang forward and knocked the cup to the floor. The water spread and darkened.

"What are you giving this gomeral a drink for? Him and Sir James are tarred with the same stick. It's the back of my hand he'll be getting."

"Sit down, Tinker." Columb's eyes met Tinker's, locked and held. It was Tinker who looked away first. "Witch, bring the man some more water. Go on, Murphy, with what you were telling us."

Murphy swallowed and edged his body as far away as possible from Tinker. "Well tonight, I just wondered, when I saw you all leaving together. You looked kind of friendly like, and so I wondered if you were maybe headed here."

"And you told Sir James what you suspected?" Christopher said.

"No, no, I swear I didn't. I wasn't certain about it."

"But you did tell O'Hare and Bowers? You said you didn't trust Master Christopher."

"Och, they wouldn't have believed me. And if I did find something, I didn't want to have to share the reward."

"Weren't you the brave one now," Witch said softly, "to come here all your lone, in the middle of the night, with the ghosts all around you."

Murphy's eyes glowed. "I was afeard all right, but gold's gold."

"What are we to do with him?" Christopher asked. "That's the question."

" 'Why, take no note of him, but let him go; and thank God you are rid of a knave,' " Finn quoted.

"Don't be talking like a fool." Tinker's voice was cold and bleak as a blizzard. "I know what we can do with him."

Murphy shivered. "You'll not be letting them hurt me, Master Christopher. If you let me go, I swear I won't tell a soul."

"You swear!" Columb said, with a snort of laughter. "Your sworn oath wouldn't be worth the breath that blew it."

"He'll have to stay here," Christopher said. "It'll mean watching him all the time, but it can't be helped."

Rat rubbed his chin with his long, thin hand. "There's a cell, Christopher. It's at the bottom of the stairs. I don't know how secure it is, but maybe we could put him there."

Christopher nodded. "Good, Rat. Let's go take a look at it."

Tinker watched Murphy balefully, and Columb watched Tinker.

"Isn't this just like it!" Tinker snarled. "Just when things were going rightly we had to have this fellow come on the scene."

"Och, aye," Witch said with a yawn. "Troubles never come single, as the old fellow said when his wife died and his hens wouldn't lay."

Christopher was smiling as he and Rat came back. "It's just right. There's an outside bolt, plenty of air, and he'll be out of our way."

Columb and Finn helped Murphy to his feet.

"I'll freeze to death, so I will," Murphy shouted. "You'll all forget about me and I'll starve to death."

"I'll not forget you." Tinker drew the point of his knife against his callused thumb. "I'll be in to visit you when there's nobody around."

Christopher threw his cloak at Murphy. "You'll not freeze, either."

Columb poked Murphy in the ribs. "You've been comfortable in his Lordship's all winter," he said grimly. "It'll not do you a haet of harm to be uncomfortable for a while, like the rest of Ireland."

Rat had rekindled the fire when they came back.

"That's a gey hard floor in there," Finn said. "I'll wager old Murphy wishes he was back in his soft featherbed this night."

"It's colder in here nor a hound dog's nose." Witch rubbed her hands together. At the sound of the word dog, Obadiah's tail thumped madly and then stilled. "Have we plenty of turf?" she asked Rat.

"Aye. I bring in a kish every morning. We'll not be running short."

Witch settled back in her chair. "Tell us now about your great plan, Christopher. Even if I'm not to be in on it, maybe you'll do me the honor of letting me listen to it."

"My plan is this," Christopher said. "We're going to steal a barge full of food."

"A barge?" Witch repeated.

"Every week, a barge goes down the Suir to Waterford town. It's full to the brim with oats and barley and wheat and corn. All kinds of things. At Waterford it's loaded on a ship for England."

Finn and Columb and Witch exchanged glances.

"So that's what was in it!" Finn breathed. "We saw it going down the river yesterday. But they have military guarding it and a big gun on the back."

"Not much wonder they have to guard it," Columb said.

"Floating all that food down the middle of poor starving Ireland and then shipping it out of the country!" His voice shook with emotion. "Jakers, but I hate the English! I hate them like man never hated man before."

"Easy, easy." Finn laid a hand on his brother's shoulder. "We're going to do something about it now. That's all that matters."

"But where does all this stuff come from?" Tinker asked. "Who owns this food that's going down the river?"

"It's the way the system works," Columb said bitterly. "The landlords are near all English—absentee landlords they're called. The tenant farmers, like our father, grow the potatoes to feed their families. The other crops are grown to pay the landlord for rent, and he sells them in England."

Witch shook her head. "Aye, it's the system all right. And you might as well look for feathers on a frog's back as for a way to change it."

Tinker looked puzzled. "But why don't the farmers eat their crops themselves if they have no potatoes and they're starving? Why do they give it to the landlords?"

Roper swished his rope gently between his knees and scowled.

"It's easy seen your father wasn't a farmer," Columb said, "or you'd know all about it. If you don't pay your rent, in money or crops, you're put out of your house. Then you just die the faster, that's all. You starve in a field or a hole in the ground."

They were all silent, remembering.

"My mother and father died in a scalpeen they dug in the bog," Rat said. "You're always put out in the end anyway. It's all the same in the end."

"And how are you going to take this barge?" Columb asked at last.

"The first thing we have to do is get three carts," Christopher said. "Rat, can you go into Ballykern in the morning and see to it? Tell them you're one of us. They know us now. They'll get them for you somehow."

"Aye." Witch grinned. "Tell them you're one of the Boys from Waterford. They'll know what you mean."

"When will the barge be going down the river again?" Columb felt excitement beginning inside him. Christopher sounded so sure.

"It depends on the tides, but I'll know soon enough." Christopher rose to his feet and stretched. "I'm going back to the manor now. The less time passes, the better the chance that Sir James won't send a search party out."

"You'll be here tomorrow night?" Rat asked. "We have a wheen more mouths to feed now and I could be using some extra food."

Christopher nodded. "You'd better get the horses into shelter for the night now. I'll walk back. Those bad redheaded boyos broke their word and kept the horses. But still, they treated me well, so we'll not complain."

"You'll catch your death of cold if you're walking," Witch said, "and you with no cloak." She took the old duncher cap out of the pocket of her breeches and offered it to Christopher. "Put this on. It'll keep your ears warm."

Christopher shook his head. "Thanks, but I'm tougher than I look. It's nice to have a girl around to think of such things!"

"I'm glad you find me useful for something," Witch muttered. "I was beginning to feel about as useful as the fifth udder on an old cow around here, not being a boyo like the rest of you!"

Rat went up with Christopher to see to the horses. Columb heard Murphy kick at his door as they passed and he heard him yell, "It's dark in here. Give me a lamp."

"We only have one lamp," Rat called back. "Are you afeared of the ghosts? I'll send Tinker in to keep you company."

Columb grinned to himself at the sudden silence.

"Who minds the fire tonight?" Tinker asked Rat when he came back.

"Me." Rat stacked fresh turf on the glowing ashes and

settled himself with his back to the hearth. "I'm sorry we've no beds," he said, "but you'll find it dry and warm and safe, so I'd say we're not doing too badly."

"A gey sight better than most," Witch said. "I'll sleep tonight. It's a powerful comfort to have a full belly!"

She curled herself on the floor with one arm around Skibbereen and her head on the dog's warm back.

Columb settled himself close to Finn. He was tired, but there was a question that needed to be asked. He asked it. "What do you think of this English boy, Rat?"

"Och, he's a decent wee man." Rat's voice was slow and warm. "You shouldn't always be nyerping at him. He's doing rightly by us and ours."

Columb wanted to think about it. He wanted to say something to Tinker about the dog, and that he was a light sleeper, but he was too tired, too bone- and mind-tired, and he drifted off into sleep.

Sometime later he wakened to the sweet wailing sound of music. He opened his eyes and saw Tinker, curled in his corner by the fireplace. He was cradling a mouth organ in his big brown hands and playing a wild, plaintive melody. It was "My Dark Rosaleen," and as he played, Columb remembered the words in his mind.

> *My dark Rosaleen,*
> *My own Rosaleen,*
> *My judgment hour must first be nigh,*
> *E'er you shall fade, e'er you shall die,*
> *My dark Rosaleen.*

Rosaleen meant Ireland, and Columb sighed as he thought again of his poor land and its people. Then he heard the soft pad of paws on hard-packed earth and saw Obadiah, attracted by the music, slink across the floor to stand by Tinker. Tinker lifted his foot in its heavy boot and lashed out. Columb was wide awake now, tensed to spring, but the big dog moved out of range. He lay down, his head between his paws, watching Tinker mournfully.

"Tinker!" It was Witch, whispering. "The dog's not afeared of you when you're like this, with the hate out of you. He'd like to be your friend, so he would."

Tinker paid no attention. His eyes stared into the flames as they must have once stared into glowing camp fires. The music kept rising and falling, full of the rushing of Irish rivers, the sweep of Irish hills. Columb saw Obadiah creep closer, but Tinker seemed not to notice. When the dog put his head on Tinker's leg and howled, sadly, his voice blending with the sadness of the music, Tinker let it stay. As the last notes died to silence, Columb saw that Rat, too, was awake and watching Tinker. Tinker's face was wet with tears.

Isn't it strange, Columb thought. No matter how hard we are, there's one thing can touch our hearts and that's Holy Ireland. And that'll be the saving of the land, or the death of it, I don't know which. His own throat felt tight and rough. He turned from the firelight and closed his eyes.

When he woke again it was much, much later. For a while he lay still, wondering what it was that had disturbed him. There was no sound in the room but heavy breathing, an occasional snore, and the soft sliding of the turf in the fire. Shadows flickered across the dark ceiling, glowed and faded. Then he heard it, faint, far away, so low that it was only a whisper of sound. Voices singing in unison, sweet as the chime of chapel bells. He sat up, the skin on his scalp tingling with an unknown terror. Rat's smile was companionable in the fire glow. His eyes gleamed pale. He motioned to Columb to be quiet.

"Sh! Do you hear them? Isn't it lovely, Com? Who could be afeared of that?"

Columb lay down again, slowly. It's not ghosts, he thought. In old places like this the wind does strange things in the cracks and gaps in the stones. It just sounds like singing. It's a trick of the night and the dark and the quiet.

He lay on his back and listened. And listening, it seemed that all the misery and loneliness and fear of hunger and sickness and death faded and were gone. His last thought before he drifted off to sleep again was the remembrance of Rat's words — "I don't feel so lonely, like." And he smiled to himself in the warm, music-filled, friend-filled darkness.

9

A BARGE TO ROB

Columb lay on his stomach behind the tangle of tall, wet weeds that bordered the river path. Beside him, Roper crouched motionless, his coil of rope circling one shoulder. It was four nights since Christopher had told them his plan for robbing the barge, and now was the time.

It was snowing again, big, heavy flakes that melted on their jerseys and soaked through to make their cold bodies colder. There was a half-hidden sickle of moon, a vague thing that blurred faintly through the thickness of the night.

On the far side of the river, Columb could see the shadow that was his brother Finn and the taller shadow that was Tinker. He wished it was Finn sharing the vigil with him, the way they had shared so many adventures before, but he had done what the English boy ordered. He was with Roper. Farther downriver, around the bend, Christopher and Rat waited with the horses and carts.

At Tinker's soft whistle both boys tensed.

"It's coming," Columb breathed. "Get ready."

They crouched, waiting. "Remember," Columb whispered, "leave the two guards to me. You get your rope on the man on the barge. If he finds us with that gun, we're finished."

Roper balanced his rope in his hands and nodded. The stiff black bristle of his cowlick was sprinkled with snow.

"Good luck," Columb said.

Now they could hear the creak and jangle of harness, the murmur of voices, and the soft swish of water against the bows of the barge. The big bulky shadow drifted into sight on the river, its outline blurred by darkness and the falling snow. Almost immediately a horse and rider appeared, and another one silhouetted behind him.

Columb and Roper waited, their eyes straining to see the rope they'd stretched across the path.

The first horse fell, throwing his rider from the saddle. The man sprawled grotesquely, one leg pinned beneath the screaming beast. Behind him, the second soldier tried to rein his horse to a stop in time, but it was impossible. In a jumble of kicking hoofs and steaming leather they were all down—the horses shrieking, the soldiers cursing and yelling and trying to free themselves.

"Now!" Columb shouted. He just had time to sense the soldier on the barge as he made to swivel the gun toward them. Then there was the hiss of rope flying through the air and the man was in the river, splashing and spluttering and croaking as he was dragged toward the shore.

On the other bank there was pandemonium too, for there had been another trip rope across the path there.

Columb picked up a rifle that was lying on the ground and advanced cautiously on the two soldiers. One had managed to free himself and was climbing stiffly to his feet.

Columb pointed the gun. "Throw down your weapon. Into the bushes. Now, move over and keep your hands above your head."

The soldier limped to the side of the path.

"How are you doing, Roper?" Columb asked.

Roper was reeling in, hand over hand. He scowled, concentrating.

On the river, the barge drifted on downstream, its bargee no doubt glad to be out of whatever had happened on the bank.

Roper pulled the soldier, dripping and bedraggled, from

the water at the same time that the soldier who had been first down crawled to his feet. Columb motioned them with a nod of his head to stand together.

Roper untied his rope and used it to bind them, all three, back to back. Then he wound the rope around a tree.

"Finn! Tinker!" Columb called, cupping his hands around his mouth. "Are you all right over there?"

"Right as rain," came the answering shout. "But Tinker wants to know can he use his knife on these two?"

Columb grinned. "Tie them up, Tinker, like you were supposed to, and let's go."

They coiled their trip ropes and helped the two horses to rise.

"I don't know," Columb muttered. "That thick over there's going to be frozen stiff by morning. Look at him!"

The soldier who had been dragged through the river lay chattering in the silence. Already his wet clothes were hardening with frost.

"*We* can't help it," Roper grunted. "Let's go."

Columb shook his head. "Untie him, Roper. We'll take him with us."

"Are you crazy?" Roper's voice was angry. "Is one prisoner not enough?"

Columb fumbled with the knots himself. "If I had to kill, I suppose I could do it," he said. "But not this way. Not when it's not necessary. We'll leave him on the barge."

They mounted the two horses and Columb pulled the wet soldier up in front of him.

"Giddy-up!"

Behind them, he heard the other two easing themselves in their ropes. One of them laughed in the darkness. "Two boys," he said unbelievingly. "That's all they were. Two half-grown boys!"

Columb smiled. Half-grown or not, they had done it.

At the bend of the river they reined their horses to a walk. Columb peered ahead. "I hope the dam held!"

"It'll have held," Roper said. "When the boyos do a thing they do it right."

They laughed together companionably. Columb felt a sudden warmth, a closeness to the other boy. Roper was all right.

The big barge drifted helplessly in the middle of the river, its snubby plow bumping gently against the two giant trees that blocked the river.

"Felled by a mighty blow," Columb said softly. "Faith and they'll have trouble moving those two tree trunks, for we had trouble enough putting them there."

The barge was a ghost ship, thick, white. A silent ghost on a silent river.

Christopher and Rat appeared from the bushes. They looked like two melting snowmen, built earlier and abandoned.

"Hurry up," Christopher said. "This thing's going to take forever to unload." He caught sight of the soldier on Columb's horse. "Who's this?"

"I couldn't leave him to freeze to death," Columb said. "Even though he is an Englishman."

"No." Rat nodded. "I couldn't have, either."

"Nobody's saying you should." Christopher's voice was curt. "But now he's had a good look at me and that's something I was trying to avoid."

A shout from the opposite bank told them Finn and Tinker had arrived.

"Get a line on that barge, Roper, and we'll pull it over," Christopher said.

Finn and Tinker were crawling across the big tree trunks that spanned the river, toward the barge. They slipped and slithered on the icy surface, knocking off big chunks of hard snow that fell with soft plops into the dark water.

Roper swung and threw. The end of the rope curled and lay like a dead gray snake on the white deck before it sank into the soft cover of snow. Finn leapt aboard and secured the rope around the cabin roof. "Pull away," he called.

The four of them hauled, and the barge drifted easily toward them.

The fat bargee stumbled from the cabin with Tinker behind him. Tinker's knife was in his hand, and it seemed to Columb, even at that distance, that he could smell the bargee's fear. "Do as you're told and you won't get hurt," he called.

"Ow!" the man yelped, leaping forward so quickly that he lost his footing and fell on the deck.

"Careful with that knife," Christopher shouted sharply. "He'd like the chance to use it, would Tinker," he muttered to Columb. "He's a good boyo, but too bloodthirsty for my taste."

"I'm just letting some air out of this fat windbag." Tinker's voice was gleeful.

"Never mind that," Christopher said. "Let's get started."

Columb pushed the wet, shivering soldier ahead of him.

"Now look here," the bargee said, in a voice meant to be angry but too quavering for the proper effect. "Whatever it is that's going on here, I want no part of it." In the faint lamplight from the cabin they could see that his red face was puckered like that of a baby about to cry. "Just let me go. I won't say anything."

Columb pointed to the shaking soldier.

"Find this fellow something to put on and we'll talk about it."

When the soldier was wrapped up in a warm brown army blanket, Roper tied him and the bargee together and locked them inside the cabin.

"Hey!" the soldier shouted, his voice drifting across the water. "You—the redhaired one! The one they call Columb! My name's Crum. I'm thankful to you for what you did."

The others heard it as they huddled together on the bank.

Christopher slapped his arms across his chest to keep warm. "All right," he said, "let's get to work."

The snow was still falling and the sky was dark and heavy. Somewhere beyond the somber clouds the sickle moon lurked, but its glow was hidden from the earth's night.

"Can we have a light?" Finn asked. "You can't see your own breath in this dark."

Rat went for the hurricane lamp in the cabin. By its light they undid the waterproof covers and tilted the snow off them into the river. Then they examined their haul.

"Jakers," Columb said. He wiped the wetness from his face with the back of his hand. "That beats Bannagher, so it does!"

Jute sacks of corn and meal and grain and oats were piled, six deep, one on top of the other. Sturdy wooden barrels, metal banded, and packing cases lashed with thick ropes were stacked in the hold beside boxes of all shapes and sizes.

"Is all of that food?" Tinker whispered. "If it is, there's enough here to feed the whole country."

"That's the idea," Christopher said. "That's why we've taken it."

Columb muttered something under his breath.

"What's that?" Finn asked.

"I said, 'May God forgive them, for I can't.' One miserable sack of that meal in our house would have seen us all through the bad time. They might still be alive, Mother and Father." The wet on his face was not all from the snow.

Finn came across to stand by his brother. "There's plenty more still has the need of it. Let's get it out of here."

Side by side they worked through the night. The snow fell continuously and a damp cold crept from the river. Their shadows moved and lengthened eerily in the midnight whiteness. They rolled barrels and slid cases from the barge and hefted them onto the waiting carts. Slowly, gradually, the carts filled and the barge emptied, rising higher and higher in the water. Occasionally the horses whinnied and stamped in misery, their heads lowered against the swirling snow. Still the boyos worked on. Their backs ached and their hands and feet were numb and lifeless. Sometimes one or the other of them would stop work and rub his cramped muscles before starting again to the seemingly endless job. Tired and half frozen, in an emptiness that was mindless, they worked through the padded snow silence of the night.

"That's all we can take," Christopher said finally. "The horses can't pull any more."

"How long have we been at it, do you think?" Finn asked, as he lifted the back of the last cart and bolted it securely.

"I think it's probably about two in-the morning." Christopher stretched. "That would make it four hours."

"The barge will have been missed by now. They'll be sending somebody to see what happened."

Christopher untied the rope and pushed the barge, watching as the current caught it and pulled it back to the middle of the river. "Not for a while they won't," he said. "They got a message at Cullintra. It seems the cargo wasn't ready. These careless Irish, you know. They're a hopeless lot. You just can't depend on them for anything!" He shook his head sadly.

"You're a rare duck!" Finn thumped Christopher on the back. "I'm thinking you were cut out for a life of crime and missed your calling!"

Christopher grinned. "I am getting pretty good training here with the Boys from Waterford. I'll be a dab hand when we're through."

Columb came to stand wearily beside them.

"You're even beginning to talk like an Irishman," Finn told Christopher, "and I'm jakered, but sometimes you seem to think like one too! That was good planning—a good job."

Christopher looked quickly at Columb.

Columb turned his head away. It was a good job and the English boy had set it up well. Why then could he not warm to him? Why could he not forget his Englishness and take him for a friend? He didn't know. "We're not home safe yet," he said. "Let's stop talking and get going."

They took turns leading the horses. After some consideration they had freed the two animals the soldiers had been riding and let them go. As Christopher said, no point in making the poor beasts stand around all night if they could find shelter for themselves. It was heavy going. The carts rolled unevenly over the snow-covered ground and they had to stop every few minutes to ease the wheels out of the potholes and icy ridges.

"One good thing," Finn said. "Our tracks will be well hidden. They'll have trouble following us, come morning."

Christopher nodded. "That was lucky. I'd forgotten about tracks. I don't know how we would have covered them."

"Aye. We'd have been banjaxed for sure."

They were ankle deep in the soft snow, and tired as they were, it seemed that the way back to the abbey was fifty miles instead of three.

"I wonder how Witch is doing up in the tower," Rat said. "She'll be gey cold by now, poor wee thing."

"She didn't think that was much of a job we gave her," Columb said. He smiled, remembering. "But it's as hard as any and important too. It would be a sad thing to run into somebody before we get there."

They met no one on the road. The driving, swirling snow hid them almost from each other. They were too weary to talk, and the steady creak and pull of the carts crackled loud in the silence. Suddenly, the gray shape of the abbey was before them, blurred and indefinite in the white night.

"Wasn't Witch supposed to wail from the tower the minute she saw us?"

"Aye, but maybe she still can't see us."

They moved closer.

"She's likely asleep up there," Tinker said uncertainly. "It's powerful late."

"Or it was too cold for her to stand and she went down to the fire," Finn suggested.

Columb was silent. No, no, he thought. Please. Nothing bad to have happened to Witch!

"Something's wrong," he said, voicing the fear, unable to keep it inside. "I feel it." They stopped and stared up at the abbey.

It was so still that it seemed to Columb he could hear the snow falling. "Aye, something's wrong all right."

"Roper, you come with me," Christopher said. "Tinker, give me your knife. The rest of you stay here. If there's trouble, save yourselves and the food, if you can. If we're not back in five minutes, get out of here."

In a few seconds, their two figures vanished into the darkness. Columb and Finn and Rat and Tinker waited uneasily. The horses stood, their heads hanging with weariness and their backs steaming.

Columb huddled his chin into the collar of his jersey and blinked the snow from his eyes.

Christopher's voice, when it came, echoed eerily through the white silence. "Bring the carts in."

They pulled on the reins again and urged the horses forward.

Roper and Christopher stepped from the darkness.

"Where's Witch then?" Columb asked.

"Witch has gone," Christopher said grimly, "and so has Murphy. Skibbereen was locked in Murphy's cell, crying his heart out, and the dog's either dead or unconscious. Murphy's probably at Blunt Manor right now looking for that reward, and I think he's got Witch with him."

10

WIND GHOSTS

When the boyos had left the abbey, Witch had felt a dull resentment.

"Leaving me here," she muttered under her breath, as she scoured out the old black pot and put it to hang again on its ring by the fire. She looked around the big room that seemed empty now that the boyos were gone.

"Standing here, doing nothing, with both my legs the one length!" she muttered again. "Oh well, what can't be cured must be endured and I'd best make the best of it."

Skibbereen was sitting on the floor building castles out of the square brown pieces of turf. As fast as he built one up, Obadiah knocked it over with his nose. Patiently then, Skibbereen would start over again.

Witch smiled. "Skibbereen, you and me'll go and pick some of those good-looking nettles that are growing outside and we'll make a potful of soup for the boyos coming back. They'll be needing something hot, I'm thinking, after that caper."

She laced Skibbereen's boots on his feet and wound his muffler tight about his neck. "Have you ever picked nettles before? Well, the trick to it's to grab them tight. That way they don't sting you at all at all. You watch Witch and she'll show you the way it's done."

Obadiah rubbed himself against her legs and wagged his tail.

"All right. You can come too, you big paghill."

She found a rag to put the nettles in, pulled her duncher cap over her ears, and took Skibbereen's hand. "This is about all those boyos think I'm good for," she grumbled, "looking after the wean and walking the dog. Stay close to Witch now, for it's gey dark along the passageway."

When the voice spoke in the silence, Witch nearly jumped out of her skin.

Skibbereen tightened his grip on her hand and whimpered softly.

"Murphy! You near put the heart across me. I forgot you were in there."

"Aye, I knew it." Murphy's voice hung in the darkness. "You forgot about me. There's not one of you asked me if I had a mouth on me since this morning, and me dying of hunger."

"Stop your nyerping, Murphy." Witch's voice was sharp. "You'll be fed. And don't go talking to me about dying of hunger. I've seen it happen too many times to take it lightly." She pulled the ring that slid the heavy stone across and they stepped outside.

The last light of day was leaving the sky and the towers of

the abbey stood darkly against the lowering clouds. Witch shivered. "There's going to be more snow. The boyos will have a long, cold wait."

The spiky, green nettles grew in great clumps against the walls of the abbey.

"Sit you down, Skibbereen, and watch the way Witch takes a hard grip on these spalpeens. See, you don't need to be afeared of them if you just handle them right. It's well seen nobody comes around here or these wouldn't be left, with the hunger that does be in the countryside."

Obadiah skittered after a shadow and Witch called him sharply back. "Don't you go and get lost on me or we'll both be in a heap of trouble!"

The pile of nettles grew in the rag as Witch worked. Now it was almost completely dark. Witch straightened her back and looked at the sky again.

"It'll be night in a minute. We've got enough here for a good pottage." She lifted Skibbereen off the wall where he had been sitting. "Are you cold, Acushla? We'll get a—" Her voice trailed away. "Whist, what's that?"

There was a soft murmuring noise, like the slide-shuffle of slippered feet along the pathway or the whispering of long robes against snowy ground.

Witch crouched down against the wall and pulled Skibbereen beside her. Obadiah started to growl deep in his throat, and his ruff stood up straight and stiff like a bright orange scrub brush.

"Sh!" Witch circled the dog's neck with her arm.

Along the cloisters, from the refectory toward the abbey, the sound moved like a kindly wind in the fading light. And with it came a faint, strange, sweet-spice smell, like dying flowers or drifting incense. Witch felt the dog twitch under her arm, and then he whined a high, keening moan of terror. The sound was now loud as the rustle of autumn leaves on a hundred birch trees.

"Saints preserve us!" Witch whispered. "It's the ghosts. It's the ghosts of Kildoran Abbey."

Then the wind rose and it sounded like voices singing—

rising and soaring, echoing off the sacred stones till the night seemed full of music. And suddenly Witch felt her fear leave her as quickly as it had come.

Skibbereen whimpered and hid his face in Witch's lap.

"Hush, Acushla. There's nothing to be afeared of. It's just the wind bestowing a song upon you." She stroked Skibbereen's hair. "Come, we must get back."

As they walked down the passageway to the warm, firelit room, they could still hear the wind music, rising and falling in the night.

Witch chopped the nettles and put them with water to simmer in the big black pot. She thought about the boyos. "They'll be all right," she assured herself. "But I'd better get the wean to sleep and go up in the tower."

She poured gruel into the dish for Skibbereen. "You eat this, and then Witch is going to sit with you till you fall asleep." She filled another dish for herself and one for Murphy. "You'll get what's left," she told the slavering dog. "The rule's still 'People first, dogs after.' "

She took the hurricane lamp and carried Murphy's plate carefully to the door of his cell.

"Murphy," she called, "get away over in the far corner where I can keep an eye on you. I'll put the gruel inside the door." She held the lamp up high so that its light shone into the cell. "Murphy!"

The man lay crumpled on the floor. His eyes were closed and he was breathing heavily.

"What's the matter with you?" Witch's voice was sharp. "Now don't be trying to fool me. If you think I'm going in there for you to grab aholt of me, you're wrong. I'm not as green as I'm cabbage-looking.

She opened the door cautiously and set the plate inside. Then she locked and bolted the door again.

Murphy didn't move.

Witch shrugged her shoulders. "It's your loss. But don't complain to me about not getting fed."

It was one thing to tell herself not to worry about Murphy

and another thing entirely to keep him out of her thinking. She busied herself about the kitchen, setting it to rights. Skibbereen and Obadiah were soon asleep, curled together before the fire. Witch sprinkled water over a few pieces of turf and banked them at the back of the flames. That should keep it till I'm back, she thought. They'll be safe and dry here.

She picked up the lamp and started along the passageway again. Faintly, in the distance, it seemed she could still hear the strange, sweet wind music.

She held her lamp up and looked at Murphy through the cell bars.

He lay in the same position and the gruel sat where she had left it. A thick flaccid skin covered its surface. Murphy's breathing sounded worse than before.

Witch considered. It might be a trick. She took the lamp and determindedly went on. No use trying to outguess Murphy. She had enough on her mind as it was.

The tower was dark and cold beyond belief. Witch peered through the falling snow in all directions and saw nothing. She yelped experimentally through the funnel and scared herself so that she felt pleased with the results. Then she settled down to wait.

The tower, like the rest of the abbey, was crumbling with age and disuse. There was a roof of sorts, but the snow drifted through and blew against her numb face and her hair.

She moved around, dancing a little jig to keep warm, singing some old come-all-ye's to keep herself company. Even the wind ghosts had gone. She had no way of judging the time, for up in the dark tower it seemed that there would never be morning. She thought about her mother and father, and her brothers in America. She thought about Com and Finn and Rat, with his sweet smile, and bad-tempered Tinker who could play such gentle music and who could weep for love of his own land. And she thought of Skibbereen. What horrors had he seen that had driven the voice from his mind? And Roper, who spoke almost as little as Skibbereen but who could make his rope do his talking for him. And she thought of Murphy. And uneasiness began to gather and strengthen in her and she knew that she would have to go down and see if he was all right.

She took the lamp and retraced her footsteps through the cloisters and along the passageway. Isn't it strange, she thought. Here's me, Ryan O'Callahan, walking by myself in a place that's supposed to be full of ghosts, and knowing no fear at all at all! It's remarkable altogether.

Murphy lay in the same position, but something was different.

Jakers! Witch's mind scurried in panic. I don't hear him breathing. Maybe he's dead. She set the lamp on the floor and with trembling fingers pulled back the bolt. Slowly she moved over to where Murphy lay.

She bent over him and put her hand on his forehead. "He's dead as a herring, so he is," she muttered to herself in dismay.

"Yah! Got you!" With one quick spring Murphy was on his feet. "Now, my fine lady, we'll see who's boss around here." He twisted Witch's arm so hard that she cried in pain. "Come on, move. I'm in a hurry." He pushed her ahead of him down the passageway.

Skibbereen still slept, his cheeks flushed and slightly damp. Obadiah unwound himself and stood.

"Obadiah! Help me! Get him!" Witch yelled.

The big dog's ears flattened against his head and he padded toward them on his broad, splayed feet. Then his lips drew back from his teeth and he sprang.

In one movement, Murphy hurled Witch at the dog so that they collided and tumbled heavily on the floor. Before either of them could get up, he lifted one of the heavy wooden chairs and brought it down with a crash on the dog's head.

Witch watched in horror. The chair had splintered and broken and Murphy held one of the thick legs in his hand.

"You've killed him!" she screamed.

Murphy smiled. "Aye. Good riddance."

Skibbereen was awake and sitting up, his thumb in his mouth, his face dazed and blank with sleep. He ran to Witch and held on to her legs.

"Get back in the cell, the both of you," Murphy said. "And

don't be planning any tricks, my fine lady, or it'll be the worse for the boy."

Witch picked up Skibbereen and carried him in her arms. Above his head her eyes met Murphy's contemptuously. "Aye, you're a big man, Murphy. Powerful strong against a girl and a child. I didn't see you so high and mighty when the boyos were around. 'Don't be letting them hurt me, Master Christopher,' " she mimicked. "Oh aye, you were the brave man then!"

Murphy's face flushed angrily: "Less of your back chat, miss. Put that boy in the cell. You're coming with me. Sir James will want to know all about what's going on here, and you're the very one to tell him."

Skibbereen wound his arms so tightly about Witch's neck that she couldn't get loose. "Skibbereen, Skibbereen, Skibbereen," he whimpered, his eyes wide with terror.

"Look, Murphy, let me take him with us. He'll be afeared here on his own. I'll carry him."

"No. He'd slow us down. He stays here."

Witch placed the little boy gently on the floor and knelt beside him. "Listen," she whispered. "It won't be long till Rat and Com and the others get back. Don't be afraid, Acushla. Witch has to leave you, but you won't be alone for long." She wiped the tears from his eyes with her hands and kissed his black curls. "Can we at least leave him the lamp? He's only a wee fellow."

"No. We need it ourselves. Come on, we're wasting time." Murphy dragged Witch out of the cell and bolted the door. Skibbereen's sobs followed them all the way along the dark passageway.

Outside, the snow was falling heavily. Murphy pushed Witch ahead of him toward the manor.

Poor boyos, Witch thought. They don't know it's all over before it's begun. And poor people of Waterford. It's likely all over for them too. Och, sure the boyos were right not to trust me for I've made a mess out of the whole thing! She tried not to think of the dog lying still on the floor, or of Skibbereen, alone and frightened and weeping in the dark cell. Instead, she concentrated with all her might on how she could stop Murphy before he got to the manor.

ALONE ON THE BOREEN

The driving snow was at their backs, and Witch thought with despair that it wouldn't take them long to reach the manor. She dragged her feet and tried to make as heavy going of it as possible.

"Come on, get a move on." Murphy gripped her arm with fingers that bruised even through her jersey. "It'll do you no good to try and waste time."

Witch sensed that he was nervous. She looked at him through her eyelashes and grinned. "The boyos have horses. They'll catch up with us as sure as shooting. Ah, Murphy, I'm thinking they'll not go as easy on you this time. They'll likely take Tinker's advice on it when they get you back."

Murphy's fingers tightened. "I want none of your crack. Just keep walking."

The bog road blurred whitely ahead of them, five miles of it, stretching all the way to the manor. Now and then the faint sickle moon shafted weakly through the clouds and falling snow.

"Aah!" Witch yelped. She stumbled to her knees, her mouth twisted with pain. "I've hurt my foot, so I have." She moved heavily and sat on the road, rubbing her ankle and groaning. "I'm not codding you, Murphy. Look! Look at that great pothole that I stuck the whole of my foot in." She bit her lip, holding in the pain. "It's powerful sore, so it is."

Murphy's voice shook with anger. "Get up, miss. You give me any trouble and you'll feel the back of my hand."

Witch unlaced her boot and pulled it off. "Ow! Would you

look at that, Murphy? It's all swelling up. You can see it, as plain as a pikestaff."

"Put that boot on. You're going to walk, miss, for I'm not leaving you here to go hobbling back to the abbey, and you're a sight too big for me to carry." He pulled her up.

Witch balanced herself on one foot and cradled her boot in her hands. "Murphy," she said, and in spite of herself her voice quivered, "I'll tell you the way it was. I was just wondering how I could slow us down and I was thinking up all kinds of tricks, but begob, this is real. I didn't do it on purpose, so I didn't, and I'd just as lief not stay here my lone, but I can't walk, and that's the truth of it."

She put her foot in its old black sock down on the ground and cautiously leaned on it. "Aah—I can't do it, Murphy, and there's the end to it."

Murphy watched her with narrowed eyes. Then his hand came up and hit her hard across the face. Witch staggered and fell in the snow.

"You'll walk, I tell you. I haven't got as close as this to the reward for it to be taken from me by a play-acting besom."

Witch knocked the snow off her duncher cap and put it back on her head, cramming her long, black hair beneath it. Her face throbbed, the pain spreading all the way to her neck and shoulder. "Sorra take you, Murphy," she said mildly. "You've a terrible temper on you." She sat down on the snow again and huddled her arms about her. "You can hit me from now to kingdom come, but it's just not in me to walk on that foot. Here I am, and here I stay unless you carry me. Look!" She lifted her ankle for him to see. The movement sent sharp shivers racing up her leg. "It's as big as a bap already, and getting bigger every minute."

Murphy grunted and held the lamp higher. The ankle was puffed and shiny, the blue tinge spreading like a stain across the skin.

"Huh! It's hurt right enough. But I don't put it past you to have stepped into that pothole on purpose."

Witch felt light-headed. I've done it, she thought. I've

stopped him, or slowed him anyway, even if it was by accident. She looked innocently at Murphy. "Well now," she said. "I'm not much for bravery and I don't think I could have hurt myself intentionally. But isn't it remarkable how the angels do be taking over for us just when we need them the most?"

Murphy chewed at his thumbnail. "I'm not leaving you here. Foot or no foot, you'd get back to the abbey somehow, even if you had to crawl." He pulled her roughly to her feet and put his arm around her waist.

"Och, Murphy," Witch said primly, "and me so young!"

Murphy's voice was tight with anger. "Don't be giving me any of your smart talk, miss, unless it's another slap you're wanting. Put your arms across my shoulders."

They hobbled a few steps.

"Maybe if you'd break me a stick off one of those bushes it would help me along a bit," Witch suggested.

"Aye. And maybe you could hit me over the head with it too, first chance you got."

"Aye, maybe I could." Witch's breath came in short aching gasps, and she bit her lip to keep from groaning. Her sock was soaked through and her foot numb. The pain in her ankle was shooting into her leg, burning it, so it seemed on fire and icy cold at the same time. The boot that she carried felt heavy as a stone. The lantern swung from Murphy's hand, lightening and spreading the darkness around them. The only sound was the slow crunch of their boots and Witch's shuddering breath.

They had stumbled along for about fifteen minutes when she stopped. Murphy's grip on her waist was all that kept her from falling.

"Murphy," she whispered, "if you kill me right here, I can't go another step. Do what you want, I won't move."

This time, when he hit her, she felt the warm salt taste of blood on her mouth.

"Get up!"

"I can't."

When he hit her the second time, she lay on the ground,

her arms across her head, waiting for the kicks she knew were coming. Instead she felt Murphy drag her upright. Then he knelt in front of her. "You'll live to regret this night's work," he said. "I promise you that. Get on my back. I'm carrying you."

Without the slightest hestitation, Witch, with all the strength she had left, brought her old black boot down on the top of his head. For a second, she thought in despair that it was no use, and then, without a sound, Murphy toppled over and lay at her feet.

She righted the lamp where it had fallen from his hand and set it on the ground. Her ankle throbbed violently, and all at once she felt her stomach rebel. Jakers, she thought, swallowing hard, how did I do it, and her belly heaved again as she remembered the dull thud of the boot on Murphy's head. Frightened, she bent over him.

He was breathing normally and looked almost comfortable, his head pillowed on a hard pile of snow. Witch felt reassured, and then she thought, what if he wakes? I don't think I could hit him again. She took the lace from her boot and with difficulty tied his hands together. She thought for a second, then unlaced her other boot and bound his feet. Now that the immediate need for action was over, she was drained of all feeling and terribly depressed. She sat down beside Murphy and tried to think. How long would it be before the boyos got back to the abbey? How long before they got here? She judged she and Murphy had come no more than a mile and a half. How long before they would get here?

The snow seemed to be falling more heavily now, and already Murphy's clothes were covered with it. Witch brushed it off. She shook the hurricane lamp and was relieved to hear the gurgle of oil inside. At least, she thought, I'm not to be left in the dark. There was no sound anywhere. It was as though the whole of Ireland lay sleeping under a white eiderdown. Witch shivered. She pulled off her sodden sock and packed snow around her foot. How long?

It might have been five minutes later, or thirty-five, when

she heard the footsteps. Someone was coming and coming fast along the bog road.

Witch struggled to stand, and listened. Whoever it was was heading for Ballykern or the manor. Could it be one of the boyos? Would one of them have come alone and on foot? She wondered if she should blow out her lamp and try to hide. But what good would that do? Whoever it was was bound to see Murphy, for he lay right on the road and she hadn't the strength to hide herself, never mind him. She stood by Murphy and waited, the lamp at her feet.

A man's figure moved into the light. He shielded his eyes from the lamp glow and stopped.

"What's this?" he asked. "What's happened here?"

Witch's heart sank, for his voice was the voice of an Englishman.

He moved over to Murphy, examined him briefly, and then turned to Witch. "All right, young fellow. What are you up to? Were you robbing this man?"

Witch shook her head.

The newcomer was about thirty years old. He was big, and tough-looking, dressed in navy blue breeches, a thick blue jersey, and a woolen cap with a tassel on it.

Witch opened her mouth to answer him, but nothing came out. For once in her life she hadn't a thing to say.

The man grabbed her arm.

"I'm on my way to Blunt Manor. You'd best come with me. I'll carry him." For the first time he seemed to notice Witch's foot. "What's the matter with you?"

Witch took a deep breath. "Well, you see sir—"

"Wait a minute." The man walked over to her and pulled the cap from her head. "You're not a boy."

"No." She paused. "This man here, he was kidnapping me, so he was. And then I hurt my foot, and I hit him over the head with my boot and tied him up. And then you came along." Witch's voice trailed into silence.

"Where was he taking you?"

"To the manor."

"Why?"

"Well, you see, he wanted me to tell Sir James something that he thought I knew."

"And do you know something Sir James should be told?"

"No, indeed not, sir. I know nothing at all at all."

The man rubbed his chin. He stood deep in thought. "This thing he thought you knew. Would it have anything to do with the robbery of a barge?"

Witch struggled to keep the surprise from her voice. "A barge? What barge?"

The man watched her closely.

Witch thought, It's all over. It's out of the frying pan and into the fire for me!

"You'd better tell me all you know," the man said. "I was just on my way to the manor myself, to inform Sir James." He held the lamp high so that its light fell on her frightened face. "And just what part did you play in this night's robbery?"

12

A DEBT REPAID

Columb knelt beside Skibbereen. The little boy's face was dirty and tear-stained. He sucked his thumb and from time to time a dry shuddering sob shook his body.

"Did the man take Witch?" Columb asked gently. Skibbereen nodded, his big brown eyes solemn and dull.

"Did he hurt her?"

Again Skibbereen nodded. A cobweb was entangled in his black curls and it shimmered and danced in the lamplight.

"When did they leave? Was it long ago?"

The little boy looked puzzled.

"Had you been locked up for a long time?"

At the mention of being locked up, Skibbereen started to cry again.

Columb laid his hand against the little one's cheek. "Hush. It doesn't matter." He looked wearily at Tinker. "It's no use. He doesn't know, or if he does, he doesn't know how to tell us."

Roper had rekindled the fire and was heating Witch's nettle soup in the big pot.

Rat and Finn bent over Obadiah.

"He's bad," Rat said. "He has a cut on his head that goes from ear to ear."

Tinker brought over a bowl of water and tore a piece from the tail of his shirt. "He'd no call to do that to the dog," he muttered. "He was a decent enough beast, as dogs go."

"Aye," Finn said. " 'A very gentle beast, and of a good conscience.' " He wiped the matted blood from the dog's head, rinsed the wound clean, and probed the gash with his fingers. "It's long," he muttered, "but I don't think it's deep. Give me a hand, Rat."

They carried the unconscious animal over to the fire and laid him gently in front of it.

Christopher was drinking a bowl of soup. He had spread his cloak in front of the turfs and it steamed gently. "I need one of you to come with me," he said. "We're going after them."

"Me," Columb said. "Come on. What are we waiting for?"

Christopher hesitated. "I'd rather have Roper with me, Com. His rope might come in useful."

"All right, then," Columb said. "Roper and I'll go. You stay here."

"There's no use you showing yourself, Christopher, in case there's people looking," Finn said. "Let Com and Roper do it."

Columb pulled his knife from his pocket. "If he's hurt Witch, he'd better start saying his prayers."

Rat spoke in his slow, warm voice. "Don't worry, Com. He'll surely not have harmed her, and her only a wee girl."

Christopher's face was grim. "Take two of the horses. The poor beasts are exhausted, but it will still be a lot faster than on foot. We'll get everything hidden away down here while you're gone."

In almost complete weariness Roper and Columb un-hitched the horses and started off. Roper's coil of rope was loose across his shoulder and his scowl was as black as the winter sky. The horses, freed from the weight of the heavy carts, seemed willing enough to go after their short rest. The snow drifted down, thick as curdled cream, silent as cats' paws. Part of the way they had traveled that night already, from the river path to the bog road, but their tracks were already covered and it looked as though no man since the beginning of time had trodden across the smooth snow.

"What's that?" Roper reined his horse to a stop and pointed to a faint glow of light moving ahead of them.

"It's them," Columb said shortly. "Who else would be out here on a night like this?" In the stillness he could hear the soft whisper of sound as Roper moved his rope from his shoulder to his hand. "Or it could be searchers on the way to the abbey, looking for us."

They urged their horses on, slowly now, aware of danger.

In a few seconds they could see that only one figure was silhouetted against the night sky—a big, ungainly figure moving awkwardly with a lamp held high off the ground.

"He's carrying her." Columb scratched his head. "Now why would he do that? And even stranger, they're coming toward us. It couldn't be Witch carrying him, could it?"

They got down from their horses and moved silently to the side of the road. Columb's knife was in his hand and Roper swung his rope gently, dangerously.

"Murphy," Columb called. "Stop right where you are. We're taking you back to the abbey."

Witch's voice came faintly across the snow. "Thanks be to Kathleen ni Houlihan, it's the boyos." Then, louder and stronger. "Is that you, Com? Now don't be doing anything foolish till we get the length of you. This here's not Murphy. He's a friend, and he's helping me."

Then they were close enough to see that Witch was sitting

on a big man's shoulders and that she was the one carrying the lamp.

The man stopped in front of Columb and Roper and grinned. "My name's Crum, member of Her Majesty's First Royal Dragoons." He held out his hand and nodded toward Roper. "This fellow's good with a rope, but there's not a knot tied I can't unpick."

Columb looked at him in astonishment.

Witch was smiling gleefully from her perch, her duncher cap tilted at a rakish angle and her long black hair spilling from beneath it.

"Where's Murphy?" was all Columb could think to ask.

"Oh, you'd better go and load him on one of your horses," Witch said airily. "He's lying up the path a bit, tied up and knocked out, the very way I left him."

Columb threw back his head and laughed.

"And don't go telling me again I'm not as good as any boyo," Witch said. "There'll be a few at the abbey eating their words before this night's over!" She pointed to her ankle, and Columb could see that it was swollen and discolored. "I've got a sore foot. Can you put me on your horse, for this poor human beast I'm riding on's all worn out?"

Columb lifted her gently from Crum's shoulders and onto his own horse.

"The man's back a piece," Crum said. "Maybe a half mile. I was sent to the manor for help to get the barge moving again. The others are already working on those trees to get them off the river." He gestured to the baggy blue trousers and sweater he wore. "These belong to the bargee. A fat windbag, I think one of you called him!" He grinned and settled his cap more firmly on his head. "I'd better be getting on now or they'll wonder what's keeping me. I've seen nothing and I know nothing, except that the barge was robbed by a bunch of young hooligans."

Columb held out his hand. "We're obliged to you."

"I owed you something." Crum took Columb's hand and shook it warmly.

"One more thing I'd ask of you," Columb said, "though you've more than repaid the debt already. One of our boyos—he's English like yourself and a sort of a relative, like, to Sir James. He's helping us, do you see, but without Sir James knowing. He's back at the abbey now waiting for us."

Crum was nodding his head, understanding on his face. "You want me to be sure to give nothing away about him."

"Aye, that and more. I want you to give him time to get back to his room in the manor before you raise the alarm. It would be bad for him and for all of us if they got suspicious."

Crum smiled. "I'm a slow walker." He laid his hand for a moment on Witch's foot. "You're better than any boyo, and don't let them tell you different." Then he gave a half salute and disappeared into the snow-swirling darkness.

Columb broke the silence. "I'll start back to the abbey right away with Witch," he said, "and get Christopher started back to the manor. You take the lantern, Roper, and go for Murphy. There's no time to waste."

Roper's eyebrows were a scowling line across his face. "My lone?"

"Och, I think you can handle an unconscious man who's tied hand and foot," Witch said sarcastically. "And I can tell by the way you're smiling, Roper, that you're powerful glad I'm safe. It's warming to a body's heart the way your face lights up when you're happy."

Roper's scowl darkened. He swung himself on his horse and glared at her. "We're not all idiots around here. There's some of us only talk when there's something to be said and only smile when there's something to smile at!"

Columb turned up the wick of the lamp and handed it to him.

"He won't need that, Com," Witch said. "His bright face will light the way. Faith and with him around, a body wouldn't even want a lamp to get out to the outhouse."

Columb hid his grin. He slapped Roper's horse on the rump and climbed up on his own beast, behind Witch.

They watched Roper till he was out of sight and then

turned their own horse toward the abbey.

"Sure you shouldn't always be onto poor Roper about his face, Witch," Columb said. "He can't help it."

Witch tossed her head. "There's nothing wrong with his face; it's the look on it that 'ud turn milk sour. Wouldn't you think now that the sight of me, safe and sound, would put a smile on the face of a sucking turkey?"

Columb laughed out loud. He felt happy and lightheaded and not even tired any more. He pulled Witch's long tangled hair where it streamed down her back. "You're getting to be a conceited monkey. It's living with all these boyos that's doing it!"

"Aye," Witch said. "And it's finding out I'm better nor any of them!" She pulled her duncher cap down over her eyes to save them from the swirling snow. "Is Skibbereen all right? Was he terrible afraid, poor wee mite?"

"He's all right, and Obadiah's bravely too. And there's more food at the abbey than you've ever seen in all your born days."

"The plan worked then? You got the barge?"

"We got the barge."

Witch sighed and leaned back against Columb. "I nearly spoiled it all, Com, but I managed rightly in the end," she said contentedly. The dark, unfriendly night seemed suddenly friendly, a place for whispering together, a place for telling.

"Did I ever recount to you about my brothers?" she asked sleepily. "Brendan, he went to America first and he saved the money and sent for Eamonn, and then they saved and sent for Michael. Do you see, all the way down. I was to be the next one to go, being as how I'm the youngest and the seventh. But sure now that my mother and father do be dead and I've no house to live in, how will they know where to send to get me? But och, I suppose, me being a witch and all, I'll get there somehow in the end."

"How did you get to be a witch?" Columb asked, snuggling his chin into the warm, sweet softness of her hair. "Were you born with it, or was it something that grew?"

"Well, like I told you, Com, I'm the youngest in my family. I'm the seventh child of a seventh child and I was born in a caul. They tell me that the banshees wailed through the whole countryside the night I was born and the cows in Waterford County gave no milk for three days and three nights. That's a sure sign, you know."

Columb's voice was soft. "I've never had a witch for a friend before as far as I can mind, so I'd better make the most of the experience."

Witch's weight was sleepy-heavy against him. He thought about Crum and Christopher. He had acted instinctively to protect the English boy, to make it safe for him back at the abbey. That much he had done. But that didn't have to mean he liked him or trusted him now. Not at all at all.

The screaming, shrieking screech when it came out of the darkness startled him from his thoughts. The horse shied.

"It's all right, fellow," Columb said, leaning across Witch to soothe the beast with his hand. "It's only one of us. No need to be frightened."

Witch shivered. "Even when you know what it is, it's fearsome. It's a good hideaway we have here. It's safe, so it is."

"Aye," Columb said grimly. "It better be. I've a feeling Sir James is going to turn County Waterford upside down just looking for us. It better be safe."

13

THE BEST BEASTS
IN THE COUNTRY

Christopher undressed hurriedly and leapt into bed. His heart was still pounding from the gallop back to the manor and the mad scramble up the ivy and into his room. He heard the loud clang of the doorbell and the slow sound of Bowers's feet as he grudgingly answered the summons. He heard the bolt being drawn back and the low mutter of voices in the hallway; then the commotion as the other servants awakened, and the hesitant and gentle arousing of Sir James. He heard the shuffle of Crum's feet as he was escorted up the stairway and into Sir James's presence, and then the bellow of anger and the string of oaths as Sir James was given the news of the barge.

Christopher nuzzled under the bedclothes and grinned to himself. His bed felt warm and he wished he could stay in it. There were good things to think about. The food, safe at the abbey. Witch rescued and uppity as ever! Columb! The stubborn big redhead didn't know it himself but the gap between them was narrowing. Someday they would be friends.

The knock when it came was loud and demanding. Christopher allowed a few seconds to pass before he answered. "Yes?" His voice was muffled, sleepy, a little irritated.

"Master Christopher? Sir James wants to see you at once. He's in his bedchamber."

"To see me now? At this hour? What time is it?"

"It's four-thirty in the morning, Master Christopher. There's been a robbery. Sir James is terrible angry. You'd best come."

"All right, all right." Christopher put a dressing gown over his nightshirt and pulled some slippers on his feet. Then he unbolted his door and followed the white-faced Bowers to Sir James's room.

Sir James was sitting up in bed, his striped nightcap askew and his face the same color as his red ruffled nightshirt. He was in a rage such as Christopher had never seen before. He kept right on talking as he waved Christopher to stand beside him. Crum, cap in hand, stood at the foot of the bed.

"And you tell me they got away with near half of the cargo? And where were you at the time, and the rest of the escort? Not tending to your business. Not protecting my property as you were supposed to be doing. Why, I'll have you all court-martialed, every single one of you. Five armed men and a cannon! By all that's holy, I'll see to it that you go to the stockade—that you—" He sputtered and coughed and wheezed with anger.

Christopher poured a glass of water from the carafe on the nightstand and held it to Sir James's lips. "Now, now, my dear gentleman, calm yourself, I pray you. Such excitement can only do you harm."

Sir James swallowed with obvious difficulty, his beady eyes bulging over the top of the glass. "You hear this?" he whispered to Christopher. "All my profits gone. Stolen from me by a gang of boys, a band of hooligans, thieves, stealing from honest men. I'll get them. I'll see to it that they're caught and put where they belong." He stared hard at Crum, who was shifting his feet uncomfortably and turning his cap around and around in his hand. "Describe these boys for me!"

"Well, they were just boys. Maybe fourteen or fifteen years old. There were six of them, or five, I can't be sure."

"Two of them with red hair? Big? The two of them twins?"

Crum nodded unhappily.

"The Mullens! I knew it. And now they've got other hooligans like themselves. Dirty, shiftless trash. Describe the others."

Crum shrugged. "It was dark. They were just boys."

"Hm." Sir James drummed his fingers on the water glass and looked into space. Outside, Christopher could hear the excited whispers of the servants.

"Was one of them a man, tall and thin, answers to the name of Murphy?"

Crum shook his head.

"Murphy's missing." Sir James hissed softly through his teeth, his eyes glazed with thought. Then he smiled. "Aha," he said, and his smile grew wider.

Christopher felt suddenly cold.

"Yes," Sir James said. "Yes indeed." He swung his short, stubby legs out of the bed. "Christopher! Take this man here into Trellagh and get Sergeant Raftery. Tell him what's happened. He's to send some of his men back to get the river cleared so the barge will be ready to move on. But tell him to leave the barge where it is for now. He's to guard it well. No one's to go near it till I get there. Tell him we expect to have the rest of the cargo recovered and reloaded by nightfall. And he himself is to come here with a twenty-man company." He smiled, showing his small yellow teeth. "We'll have those rabble-raisers in Trellagh jail before this day's ended."

In the short flannel nightshirt that barely covered his fat knees he should have been a comic figure, but he wasn't. He was all menace, all evil. "Go! Go! I have things to do."

Christopher and Crum rode the three miles to Trellagh in silence. The sentry on guard duty summoned Sergeant Raftery, who listened to Crum's story in amazement. Then he rubbed his hand across his stubble of beard. "It'll be the same fellows Sir James told me about before. We tried to find them, but they disappeared somewhere in the countryside. These Irish, you know. They're all tarred with the one stick. They'll give nothing away to the enemy, and we're the enemy."

"Oh," Christopher said mildly. "I would have thought Raftery was an Irish name myself."

"No, no indeed." The sergeant jumped to his feet. "English for many generations."

Christopher nodded. "Like Murphy."

"Those Mullens now, a bad lot and no mistake about it," Sergeant Raftery went on hurriedly. "Tell Sir James I'll attend to it right away and I and my men will be at the manor as quickly as possible." He coughed. "Er, has the snow stopped? I didn't think so. I expect we'll have to search every cottage in the whole townland looking for those carts, and every barn and stable to boot." He sighed and looked unhappy. "Ah, well." He opened the door. "Tell Sir James we'll be there before dawn."

The snow stopped falling just as Christopher and Crum got back to the manor. In the soft light of almost dawn it was a fairy-tale house in a fairy-tale country. The snow-covered trees seemed garlanded with apple blossoms. Mount Crae shimmered palely in the distance, its peaks blushing with the coming sun.

Crum breathed deeply. "It's a beautiful country and no mistake, but it's a heartbreaking one too. The snow covers the stink and if you don't see the walking skeletons you could think you were in paradise. I'll be glad when my duty here is over and I can get back to England."

"It's beautiful all right," Christopher said, "but I think it'll be many a day before any Englishman can say his duty to Ireland is over. We have a lot to make up for. I don't know if we ever can." He jumped off his horse. "We'd better go inside and make our report."

They found Sir James sitting at the big mahogany table in the dining room, partaking of breakfast. Deviled kidneys, lambs' livers, and sweetbreads were piled high on his plate.

The heavy jangle of harness and horses' hooves outside announced the arrival of Sergeant Raftery and his men. In a few minutes Bowers ushered the sergeant into Sir James's presence.

Sir James went on eating, his small hard eyes riveted on the food on his plate. He chewed noisily as Sergeant Raftery continued to stand to attention. "You!" He suddenly stabbed his knife in the air at the direction of the sergeant. "What kind of an outfit are you running? Five men and a cannon! I want every one of those men punished, do you hear me? I want them flogged! None of this namby-pamby stuff, confining them to the barracks and the like. Give them something they'll understand. Do you follow me?"

"Yes, Sir James." The sergeant's voice was low and embarrassed.

"Now. It's important that the stuff's found before they have time to examine it. You know what I mean, Sergeant Raftery. We're going to get those boyos and here's how we're going to do it. Sit down."

Sergeant Raftery, his spurs clanking and sword clanging, lowered himself gingerly into one of the carved mahogany chairs. He placed his helmet on his knee and managed to look humble, respectful, attentive, and intelligent all at once.

"I have already sent Bowers into Magheragh for Colonel McLean. Colonel McLean has just acquired three very interesting new companions. He was telling me about them just the other night over dinner."

Christopher stiffened.

Sir James loosened the sash across his stomach and patted himself gently to release a little gas. He smiled. "Yes, the colonel has just got himself three bloodhounds, and he tells me they are the best tracking dogs in the country—or any other country if it comes to that."

In the silence of the room, Christopher could hear the gilt clock over the mantel ticking gently and the slither of turf in the hearth.

"Why, how clever of you to think of them, Sir James." Sergeant Raftery looked happier at the prospect of one day's work where he had expected ten. "I've never worked with dogs before."

Sir James nodded. "Lead us right to them in no time at all." A vicious look tightened his face. "Just let me get my hands on them and they'll wish they had never been born."

Christopher felt his heart beat uncomfortably loud. "But, Sir James, what about the snow? How can the dogs follow a trail when it's been snowing?"

"Makes no difference to these beasts. The colonel says rain or snow or hail or sleet, nothing puts them off once they've got the scent. And there'll be plenty of scent for them to pick up around that barge." Sir James helped himself to more kidneys. "So we'll just wait for Colonel McLean to get here and then we'll be starting."

Christopher tried to speak, but he found his throat was dry.

"What's the matter, Christopher? I hope you're not catching cold. Your face looks a little white. Too bad if you couldn't come with us on our rat hunt. It should be quite an experience."

14

RATS IN A TRAP

Rat spooned cold stirabout into earthen bowls and handed them around. "I suppose we'd better take Murphy in some food," he said.

Columb grinned. "Witch would offer to take it, but she's in bad fettle the day. Murphy and her's old friends. They even walk about together, you might say!"

Witch sniffed. She sat on one chair with her sore foot propped up on another one. "You're a great one with the jokes, Com Mullen. You'll pardon me for not laughing." She leaned over and patted Skibbereen's head. "Eat your stirabout, Acushla. You need to grow. You're not the height of two dandelions wanting their heads."

Skibbereen ate a mouthful and, then, when Witch wasn't looking, fed a spoonful to Obadiah who lay beside him. Obadiah wore a piece of Witch's shirt on his head for a bandage and an ashamed expression.

In the corner the two horses huddled together and blew through their noses, for it was almost as cold inside as out.

Witch scraped the last of her stirabout from the bowl and ate it with relish. "You make powerful good stirabout, so you do, Rat. If there's any more, I'll have it, for I have to keep up my strength on account of my poor sore foot."

Columb paced up and down the room, stopping to pet the horses and to examine again the supplies stacked against the wall. He fingered the sacks. Something niggled at the back of his mind.

"I hope Christopher got back all right," Rat said, "and I hope Crum told a good story." He carried a dish full of stirabout out of the door.

Tinker slammed his bowl down on the table. "Och, you're far too trusting, the lot of you. It's only asking for trouble to keep prisoners and let them escape, and then to go saying an

English soldier won't scut on us. You should have let me go after him. I would have gutted him like a herring, him *and* Murphy!" He spat into the dead fire and the cold gray ashes powdered and scattered.

"Tinker," Witch said coldly. "You spit like that again and I'll gut YOU like a herring!"

Rat came back from Murphy's cell. "Murphy was asking for you, Witch. He says you tricked him, but he'll not be holding it against you. He says you took advantage of his good nature."

"Why that—!" Witch spluttered. "I tricked *him*! Sure he—"

A shrill scream froze them all to silence.

"It's Roper. He must see something."

The bloodchilling wail came again, long and drawn out. Then for a few seconds there was a quiet so intense that they could hear one another's breath.

"Yaaa—eee—aaaaaa!" Echoing and reechoing off the cold stone and the frigid earth, the screams were terrifying.

"It'll be that soldier," Tinker whispered. "He's leading them straight back to us."

There was the creak of the stone slab sliding back, the slither as it reclosed, and then the clatter of feet on the steps and along the passageway.

Rat unbolted the door, and Roper fell into the room.

"We're finished," he gasped. "There must be two dozen of them out there. They're heading straight for the abbey and they've got dogs with them."

"Dogs?"

"Aye, dogs that are barking their heads off and pulling the men that's holding them. They stopped for a minute when I tried to scare them off, but then they just kept on coming." He stopped, panting, his rope motionless in his hand.

Skibbereen started to cry, and Witch gathered him awkwardly into her lap, wincing as he bumped against her ankle.

"There's something else, isn't there?" Columb asked. "Something you haven't told us?"

Roper dropped his eyes and smoothed his rope with his fingers. "Aye. There's a boy with them. It's hard to tell with the snow and everything, but it looks terrible like Christopher."

"Christopher?" Witch shook her head.

"I don't believe it," Rat said. "Christopher wouldn't go agin us. If he's there, it's to help us."

"Christopher!" Columb's voice was bitter as his thoughts. "You don't believe it, Rat? Well, I do! There's nothing bad enough to believe of the English!" Anger choked in his throat, all the fiercer because, deep inside, he knew that he himself had come close, very close, to trusting.

Finn spoke into the uneasy silence. "We can't worry about that now. We've got to do something."

Columb shook his head, trying to clear it, trying to think. "Rat! Get Murphy and bring him in here. We'll have to put a gag on him. Then we'll pile everything against the door and try to hold them off, if we can. Are you sure you left no tracks, Roper?"

"Well, the snow started again, so if I did they'll be covered."

"Och, stop codding yourselves," Tinker said. "If they have dogs that got this length, they'll have no trouble finding us down here, tracks or no tracks. Dogs!" he muttered. "I always knew I'd be done in for by a dog in the end."

"Aye," Columb said. "And if someone that knows is leading them, we've no chance at all."

"What's that?" Witch's voice was scratchy-soft. Clearly, now, they could hear the sharp, staccato yelping.

"What do you think? It's the dogs, and they're getting close." Tinker drew his knife from his pocket. "Dogs!" he said again in disgust.

Columb looked around the room. "Caught like rats in a trap, and all the evidence they need right here."

"Sh!" Rat whispered. "Listen."

Witch cocked her head on one side. "I can't hear anything now."

"That's what I mean. I don't, either. I wonder what they're up to?"

15

INVISIBLE SMOKE

Christopher peered through the snow at the abbey. He wondered who had been in the tower. Tinker likely, or Roper.

When the wailing had started, the horses had hesitated and pulled back on their reins, and the three dogs had growled and raised their hackles. Everyone looked suddenly uneasy, but Sir James whipped them on with his anger.

"Are you a bunch of women?" he asked coldly when they paused. "Are you ignorant Irishmen, stupid enough to be taken in by a trick, afraid of a place just because it's said to be haunted? Look at the dogs! They know what's in there. Come on, come on."

And the dogs were indeed moving again, snuffling excitedly, with their noses half buried in the soft-fallen snow.

"Oh, Sir James," Christopher asked. "What if there are ghosts? They say it's true that the spirits of men long dead have been heard at Kildoran Abbey." He was careful to speak loudly so that all the men around him could hear.

There was a small grumble of protest.

"That didn't sound like a human cry to me, Sir James. It really did not."

Sir James glared at him with contempt. "I've put you down for a spineless fool before now," he said, "and I was right." He guided his horse to the front of the group and urged them on.

Slowly, hesitantly, with the dogs yelping and yapping on their leashes, they moved forward. The snow, which had stopped briefly, had started again, and the walls of the abbey were almost hidden by the swirling, driving frenzy.

"Just look at those dogs of yours," Sir James said to Colonel

McLean. "Those beasts are the best I've ever seen. They'll get recognition for this night's work."

He had scarcely finished speaking when the dogs came to a sudden stop, their noses quivering, their front paws half raised, as though debating another step.

"What is it?" Colonel McLean asked, dismounting and talking to them gently.

They were almost in the shelter of the south wall of the abbey where the fallen stones made a natural opening into the ruined building.

The dogs started to growl, deep in their throats, and then to whine, a high-pitched, keening whine of terror. Their bodies shivered and trembled, and the loose skin that hung in folds about their heads and necks swung wildly from side to side.

Then the horses started. They rolled their eyes and tossed their necks. Their manes blew in the wind, trapping the snowflakes, so that they looked like circus horses, pearl-studded. Then they planted their legs, stiff as blackthorn sticks, in the soft ground.

"What the—!" Sir James muttered, as he tried to control his black stallion. "Confound it! What's the matter with these animals?"

"Sh!" Christopher laid his hand on Sir James's arm. "Listen."

In the snow-muffled quiet they could hear, from behind the wall, a slow shuffle as of slippered feet. A strange, faint smell hung in the air like perfume or incense. And then, softly and gently into the snow-drifting, white-swirling silence, rose a sound. It was like a chant, like singing, like an exquisite choir. It soared and rose and filled the day, floating on the heavy air, tangling in the soft gray sky clouds.

The horses whinnied in fear, prancing backward, spilling their riders from the saddles. Most of the men were on the ground, trying to control the animals, or standing, silent, listening. A few went down on their knees in the snow.

Sir James's voice was a bluster of uncertainty. "Now look

here. It's a trick. It's only the wind blowing through the stones."

"What wind?" Christopher asked quietly. "There is no wind."

The three bloodhounds sat in the snow, their muzzles pointing to the sky, and howled dismally.

"If it's a trick, then it's got the dogs fooled all right," Colonel McLean muttered. "I've never seen them like this. They'll go no farther."

"Well, I will!" Sir James said. "Is there any among you man enough to come with me?"

The men were suddenly all busy with stirrups and halters.

"Come on, Raftery. I want you to take some of your men and go in there and search that abbey."

Sergeant Raftery looked unhappy. "Well," he said, "I don't know what for. The dogs have given up the scent. There's nobody in there."

Sir James's rage overflowed. "You crawling, miserable coward! I'll see about this. Falling down on your duty. Come along, colonel, we'll go ourselves. I know they're in there."

"Oh, not I," Colonel McLean said quickly. "I can't leave my dogs and they won't move. Look!" He pulled on the leashes but the dogs sat immovable, baying at the sky.

Sir James looked at him with narrowed eyes. "Very well. I'll go myself. I'll not be beaten by a gang of young hooligans, no, nor ghosts either." He urged his horse forward but the animal stood firm. Its ears were flat against its head and its big yellow teeth were bared in a fearful grin.

"Curse you!" Sir James kicked the horse in the ribs so that the animal screamed with pain. "I need nobody, not even you." He lowered himself awkwardly from the horse, his short legs dangling a good six inches from the ground. Then he was gone, scrambling over the mounds of snow and into the abbey.

The others watched him till the walls and a flurry of snow hid him from sight.

From somewhere the wind music rose in a spiraling crescendo.

Christopher shivered. He didn't believe in ghosts, as Rat did. He knew who was doing the haunting of Kildoran Abbey. But what on earth were the boyos doing that was making that strange, wild, eerie music?

All at once there was a hush, so absolute that it was spine-chilling. Then hurrying footsteps scrambling over broken stones and frozen snow scattered the stillness. Sir James's face was colorless as a winding sheet.

"Come on," he gasped, clawing at his horse and wheeling it away from the abbey. "There's nobody there."

"But, Sir James," Christopher said, "we heard *something*. It sounded like voices."

"Nobody, I tell you. The dogs made a mistake. We'll have to look somewhere else." He made as if to say more, stopped, and then started again. "The place was empty, save for this high music. It was like singing, but there was nobody there. Just emptiness. I tried to go through the abbey but I couldn't. There was depth, and thickness—and, and—substance to the emptiness and I couldn't get through it. It was like a wall, a wall of colorless smoke. It was in my mouth and in my throat, choking me, drowning me. . . ." His voice rose hysterically and then dropped to a whisper. "It's bad air in there. It's likely the age of the place. Invisible—smoke." His voice trailed into silence. A small sound came from his throat.

Christopher hid a smile. The sound had been remarkably like a whimper.

In the underground room the boyos waited behind the barricaded door. Murphy's eyes gleamed viciously over the tight gag. Witch sat with Skibbereen in her lap and the dog at her feet. They heard the wind music that seemed to fill the abbey, almost to fill the whole world. They heard it soar suddenly and then cease, to an aching silence.

"What is it?" Finn asked Rat.

Rat smiled. "It's the ghosts. They do be scaring them away."

Columb, remembering the night he had heard the music before, said "I'm going up there. I want to know what's happening."

He was back in a few minutes. "There's nobody there at all at all. Nobody in sight. I climbed to the top of the tower, and the whole countryside is empty as a sinner's heart."

They looked at each other in relief and wonder.

"It was the ghosts." Rat's voice was warm with love. "They went out there, and they saved us. They know."

"Aye," Witch whispered. Her small rough hands trembled as they smoothed Skibbereen's curls.

"It's easy for people to get afeared out here," Columb said. "It was likely just the wind in the stones."

His hands were clammy and he wiped them on his breeches.

Rat shook his head so his white hair gleamed in the darkness. "It was the ghosts. And they saved us. They do be Irish ghosts. Didn't I tell you all along not to be afeared of them?"

16

THE BOYS FROM WATERFORD

It was three days before Christopher came back to the abbey. Then, on the third night, they heard the stone slide across and Christopher's voice at the door, giving the password. Finn drew back the bolt.

"God save all in this room!" Christopher said, in his fake Irish accent.

Columb felt his usual anger building inside him. "Give over," he muttered.

Finn shook Christopher's hand. "We were wondering

when you would get here." His voice was warm and friendly as ever.

Columb found it necessary to busy himself at the table, his back to the room.

The fire roared in the chimney and something hot and savory bubbled in the big black pot.

Witch sat in front of the glowing turfs. She had washed her hair and she fanned it toward the heat, combing it with her fingers. "Come sit by the warm," she told Christopher. "There'll be broth soon."

Columb felt her eyes on his back. He swung around. "The dogs nearly got us a few nights back, Master Christopher. Roper noticed you were one of those leading them."

"Hush, Com," Witch began. "Sure none of us thought—"

"No, don't hush him." The color had drained from Christopher's face. "I tried to stop them." He told them what had happened. "Don't you believe me?"

"Oh course we do," Finn said quickly. He put an arm about Christopher's shoulders, and turned him from Columb's frown. "Come over here a minute till we show you what Com found."

The supplies stacked against the wall had been divided into three equal piles, ready to be moved. Finn turned one of the jute sacks toward the lamplight so that Christopher could see the big black letters stenciled on it: "V. R." And then underneath that a crown, and below the crown, in smaller black letters, "W. D."

Christopher's eyes met Finn's. "Victoria Regina," he read. "War Department. So that's what he meant when he said he wanted to find the supplies before they were seen." He told them about the conversation between Sir James and Sergeant Raftery. "His Lordship's been stealing from the government stores!"

"Aye," Finn said, "from what you say, Raftery's in on it too. Now that we know, is there any way we can make use of it?"

"Let me think about it," Christopher said slowly. "If I could get hold of my father. Or if we could tell Lord Bessborough.

He would be the only one with the power to do anything."

Finn nodded. "Lord Bessborough would be the one. They say he's a terrible good lord lieutenant and sympathetic to the troubles of the country. Could you get to him, Christopher? Does he live far from Waterford?"

"Bessborough town's in Kilkenny, about forty miles from here. I'll go tomorrow. This could be the beginning of the end for Sir James."

Columb lifted an empty sack from the table. "I took the meal from this one for us to use. You can take the sack with you when you go to Lord Bessborough. It'll be our evidence. We have fourteen more of the marked sacks here, and there'll be plenty left on the barge."

Christopher smoothed the sack with his fingers. "You trust me to go to Lord Bessborough? You trust me with the evidence, Com?"

Columb raised his eyebrows. "Do we have a choice? But don't betray our trust in you, Christopher. If you do, I swear—"

Witch ran over and put her hand on Columb's arm. "You're a hard man, Com, and there's no charity in you. It's sad, so it is."

Finn spoke quietly. "Go to Lord Bessborough, Christopher. Tell him of the good business Sir James had going for him. All pure profit, save what he gave Raftery and whoever was working with him on the other end."

"And he was likely stealing it regular," Tinker added.

Witch shook her head. "It's a powerful sad thing," she muttered. "Him as rich as cream and greedy as a gull besides!" She squeezed Columb's arm. "Och sure, the mortals of this world have a lot of failings, so they do." She laid her head against his arm to stop the angry words he had ready. "Tell us now, Christopher, what's happening in the outside world?"

"Well," Christopher said, "Sir James is fit to be tied. He wants to get you, badly, and now I can surely see why. They've searched everywhere, all over the whole countryside. They tried to use the bloodhounds again, but every time the dogs are given your scent they start howling and yelping and acting like they're going to fall down in a dead faint! Sir James has decided they're useless and McLean has fallen from favor!" He grinned at Finn. "And you and your brother are famous. There's rewards posted for you on every tree and post and wall between here and Waterford town.

" 'WANTED: for theft and for assault on members of Her Majesty's Army: the persons known as the Boys from Waterford. Columb and Finn Mullen: aged 15 years.'

"Then there's a description of the two of you and a reward of ten pounds for your capture. And three pounds apiece for any of the rest of you. You're dangerous men, so you are! But I noticed when I came through Ballykern that every one of the posters had 'Wanted' crossed out, and 'God Bless' written in. I tell you, the name of Mullen's going to be well known in all of Munster before Sir James is finished."

"Do you remember, Witch?" Finn asked.

"Remember what?"

"The very first time we met. You told Com and me that our name would be known in all Ireland, and that some would bless it and some would curse it."

Witch nodded. "Aye," she said. "Of course I don't rightly mind it, but if you say I prophesied it, then I did. I'm powerful wise, you know," she added complacently, "even if I don't remember the half of what I say."

Columb pulled her hair, his annoyance at her forgotten. "Och," he teased, "it's a pity you have such a low opinion of yourself. Wouldn't you think, now, with all of us telling you how great you are you'd begin to think a bit more of yourself?"

Roper scowled at his rope. "Conceited besom! If conceit was deadly, that one wouldn't be with us long!"

Witch ignored him. "Tell us more about what's happening, Christopher."

"Was it that Englishman, Crum, that led them to us?"

Tinker asked, his beaked nose pointing like a bird of prey.

Christopher pulled off his mittens and held his hands to the fire. "No, Crum didn't say a word. No more than I did." He glanced quickly at Columb. "It was the dogs. I never saw anything like them. They got your scent, and there was no turning them away. If you hadn't managed to scare them off, you'd have all been under lock and key by now. How did you do it, anyway?"

"It was a trick of the wind what turned out lucky for us," Columb muttered.

Rat's pale eyes reflected the firelight like mirrors, shooting off orange-gold sparks. His voice was whisper-soft.

"It was the ghosts. And they've been singing powerful sweet for us these past few nights. Tell us the words again, Finn. The ones you said the night the ghosts saved us."

Finn stared into the glowing hearth.

> *"O how comely it is, and how reviving*
> *To the spirits of just men, long oppresst,*
> *When God into the hands of their deliverer*
> *Puts invincible might,*
> *To quell the mighty of the earth, th' oppressor."*

"Sounds like the words of an Englishman by the name of John Milton," Christopher said with a smile." And when *he* talked about 'the oppressor' he wasn't meaning the English."

"Well," Columb said, "he can be oppressed by whoever he likes, but to an Irishman 'the oppressor' is always an Englishman.

Christopher nodded. "I know, Com. It's that way now. But it won't always be."

Finn spoke quickly. "What I think," he said, "is we need more of us working together, like us and Christopher. Learning about each other. Even liking each other." He rose and put his hand on Christopher's shoulder.

Witch hobbled to the black pot. "Do you want a sup of the broth now? There's a smell coming out of this that 'ud make your jaws drip!"

"Dish it up, Witch," Christopher said. "It's going to be a long night. We can't wait any longer to give out the food. The people are in worse shape than ever. Everything's picked clean and they're not even bringing in the Indian corn any more. They issued potato seed for the next planting, but the people can't wait for the potatoes to grow. They've eaten the seed, so now there's nothing to plant for the next crop. They're dying like flies in winter and there's no spirit left in them at all. They're waiting to see which comes first, Henry John Johnson or death, and they don't much care which."

The bubbling of the pot and the roar of the fire were the only sounds in the room.

Skibbereen sucked his thumb and played with Obadiah's ears. His brown eyes moved curiously from one face to the other.

Wordlessly, Rat got out the earthenware bowls and held them for Witch to fill.

"And in Ballykern?" Finn asked, and Columb knew he was thinking about old Mick.

"Ballykern's better than most." Christopher blew on his broth to cool it. "The food we took them last week has kept them going. But they need more now if they're to stay alive. I can't understand what's keeping Johnson. He was supposed to be here before now, you know, and then we got the word that he had been held up."

Columb's voice was brisk. "All right. First we take the carts up and put them together. What's it doing outside? Is it snowing again?"

Christopher shook his head. "It's clear, with a moon. I don't know if that's good or bad. At least we'll be able to see."

They ate quickly and started work.

Murphy was taken from his cell and put to carrying boxes of food to the bottom of the stairs for them to take up.

Obadiah lay by the door and unblinkingly watched his every move. He hadn't forgotten the chair across his head and he silently showed his teeth each time Murphy passed. Murphy walked warily, careful to make no sudden moves.

It took them till past midnight to assemble and load the carts. The marked sacks were piled in a corner and left behind. Then they harnessed the horses and were ready to go.

Christopher gave the last-minute instructions. "The Mullens had better split up. Com, you go with Roper to Magheragh. They'll need the whole cartload there. Knock on the cottage doors and then just leave everything in a pile. Tell them to take what they need and feed each other, the way we're feeding them. Tinker and Rat, you go to Toberone and Trellagh. Leave half in each. And Tinker, stay clear of that army barracks. Keep to the other end of town. Finn, you and I'll go to Crossgarvin and Ballykern. I wish we had more," he muttered, peering through the half-light at the three loaded carts.

"Aye," Tinker said. "Did you ever feel like somebody spitting on a burning house to put the fire out? There's so little for so many."

"There's enough for a week's life for five towns," Rat said, "so we can't complain."

Columb made sure Murphy was locked away securely and then spoke with Witch. "You'll be all right, so?"

"Right as rain. Here." She handed him her old duncher cap. "Pull this down over your ears, Com. It's gey cold out there." Her eyes were soft and green as grass. "You're a terrible fool sometimes, but what does it matter?"

Columb took the cap and rubbed it like a talisman. He ruffled Skibbereen's curls and patted Obadiah's head. "Take care of Witch and the wean," he told the big red dog. "Don't be letting anybody crack you on the head this time." Then he jammed the cap on his head and left. He heard Witch call after him, "Over your ears, I said, Com Mullen!" Columb smiled. He pulled the cap down the way she had ordered.

Witch gathered the bowls together and poured water from the bucket into the basin to wash them. Her heart was heavy at the thought of her starving people. "Faith and I don't know at all at all," she muttered, rolling up the sleeves of her old red shirt and starting on the dishes. "What'll be the end of it?

Eating the seed, the poor craters, and them in need of it for the planting!"

When the voice behind her said "Witch," she got such a fright that the bowl she was holding slipped from her hand and shattered in a hundred pieces on the floor. She grabbed another bowl off the table and swung around, arm raised to strike.

There was nobody there. Skibbereen still sat by the fire, his arms around the dog, his eyes fixed on her face. The only sound was the dog's heavy breathing and the splutter of the oil lamp.

"Aaragh," Witch mumbled to herself. "I'm beginning to dote in my old age." She dried her hands and cautiously unbolted the door. "Murphy," she shouted, ashamed at the tremble in her voice. "Murphy? Did you call out this minute so?"

"Naw! A lot of good it would do me to call out to any of you. You're a lot of unfeeling monsters, so you are!"

"Oh, aye, and you're an angel of light. I know all about that."

Thoughtfully she rebolted the door. She carried an armful of turf from the kish in the corner and stooked them on the fire. Then she sat down, rubbing her ankle, grimacing at the dull ache.

"It is bad, Witch?"

Witch's hand froze in midair.

Skibbereen sat back on his heels, watching her.

Witch slid off her chair and knelt beside him. "Acushla," she whispered. "You spoke. Real words!"

She took his shoulders in both hands and shook him in her excitement. "You spoke! Thanks be to all the saints, for they've heard my prayers." She hugged Skibbereen tight against her and cried into his silky curls. "And isn't that just like Witch, blethering away here and not giving you the chance to say anything else, and you deprived for so long! Say something for Witch. What's your name? Your real name, not Skibbereen."

112

Immediately she saw panic struggle into his face. "Skibbereen," he whispered. "Skibbereen."

"Sh, sh," she crooned, rocking him back and forth against her. "Don't worry about it now. It's enough that I know you can say something besides that; that the words are in you just waiting to come out." She held him away from her and looked into his small, white face. "Wait till we tell the boyos! What a surprise we'll give them."

Skibbereen nodded gravely and smiled. Then he put his thumb into his mouth and lay down, his head on Obadiah's warm stomach.

Witch sat looking into the fire, her mind in a turmoil. She had accepted Skibbereen's silence so completely that it was hard to believe it was over. Isn't it grand altogether, she marveled. The fear does be leaving him and the bad memories too, and now the words are coming back!

The warmth of the fire lulled her and she leaned back contentedly, watching the shadows shrink and lengthen on the white ceiling. She hoped all went well with Com and the rest of the boyos. She hoped all in the townland would eat that night.

SHADOWS

The boyos came back to the abbey, two by two, in the early light of dawn, like the animals going into the ark. All except Christopher. He came back last and alone.

Suspicion crowded into Columb's mind. "Where's Finn?" he asked, running out to lead the tired horse over the loose rocks behind the abbey walls.

Christopher rubbed his hands across his eyes.

"He stayed behind in Ballykern. I begged him to come back

with me, but he wouldn't. Old Mick's dying; he won't last till the morning. He knew Finn, and Finn wouldn't leave him."

"Och no," Columb said. "Poor old Mick! It's hard times to be old in. But all the same, you should have made Finn come with you. It will be daylight soon and that's taking too big a chance."

Tinker had come to stand silently behind them. He twisted the gold hoop in his ear so that it glittered, like his eyes, in the first lightening rays of the winter sun. "Aye, it's hard times to be old in and hard times to be young in, too," he said bitterly. "In Toberone, I saw more wee ones dead and dying than anyone else!"

Christopher climbed down from the cart and unhitched the horse. "Poor beast." He rubbed its head gently and stroked its small ears. "And now you're going to have to carry me back to Blunt Manor! Did everything go all right in Magheragh?"

Columb nodded.

"And with you, Tinker?"

"Aye. We would have been back sooner, but we had trouble finding anyone fit to carry the food. We had to take it from door to door. There's only a wheen of them's able to walk." His voice was harsh. "Faith and I'm sick of it. I'm sick of the look and the smell of hunger. Is it ever going to be like it used to be? And why was it our land that had to be afflicted?"

Neither Columb nor Christopher answered him, for there was no answer to give.

"When will you try to see Lord Bessborough?" Columb asked Christopher.

"Well, I've been thinking about that. It's going to take two days, maybe more. And I need some excuse. We'll talk it over tonight when I come back to the abbey. I'll bring more oats for the animals and whatever else I can find. And we'll plan our next job. The people still have to eat, whatever happens to Sir James, and whatever happens to him is going to take time. We daren't just sit back and wait for Johnson." In the cold dawn light he looked more man than boy. The lines of weariness on his face made him suddenly old. Columb felt a quick rush of something. If Christopher was all that he seemed, he was giving a lot to Ireland—if Christopher was all that he seemed. He slapped the horse's rump hard, knowing himself confused and unsure. "Giddy-up," he said.

The horse moved slowly, reluctantly, in the direction of the manor. Wordlessly, Columb and Tinker unbolted the side-gates and tailgates of the cart and carried them below.

Witch was fussing about. Her eyes shone with excitement. Columb could tell that she wanted to talk.

She waited till everything was done and the boyos sat down to rest. Then she told them about Skibbereen.

Columb touched the black tangle of Witch's hair. "Great altogether. And it's you, Witch, that's helping him get over the silence. He'll talk more. We just need to be patient." He yawned a yawn wide enough to make his jaws crack. "I'll be asleep in this chair in two minutes. Can you listen for Finn for me, Witch?" He yawned again and with his eyes closed murmured sleepily, "Poor old Mick. He was a good friend to the Mullens."

Finn did not come that morning, or all that day. The wind had come up, and high in the storm-buffeted tower Columb strained for the sight of the familiar figure coming along the bog road from Ballykern. But the boreen was empty. The black crows rose from the trees, throwing their voices into the wind, only to sink again, breathless on the swaying bare branches. By nightfall he was edgy with anxiety.

"What can have happened to him, Witch?" he asked when he was finally driven by darkness to join the others. "I'm going to go after him. I can't sit here when Finn may be in danger."

"Sh," Witch said, comforting him as though he were a small child. "He'll come. He'll want to stay with Old Mick till the end, and with the strong spirit the old fellow has it'll likely be a long thing. Wait till Christopher gets here and then we'll decide what to do."

She made him sit and eat a bowl of stirabout.

"Skibbereen hasn't said another word," she told him. "Do you think I'm doting, Com? Do you think I fell asleep and dreamed it?" She looked at Columb imploringly. "I've coaxed him and coaxed him, but not a holy word will he give me. It's enough to make you spit, so!"

There was a loud knock on the door.

Columb grinned. "Finn!" He rushed to open it, but the voice giving the password was Christopher's.

"Hasn't Finn come back yet?" He set the heavy saddlebags he was carrying on the floor but made no attempt to take off his cloak. "I'd better ride into Ballykern and see what happened."

"I'm coming with you," Columb said, moving toward the horses tethered in the corner.

"Better not, Com, it's—"

"He's my brother, I'm coming."

The wind had not dropped. It howled free across the bog, rattling the loose stones of the abbey, screaming through the broken walls and bending the bare trees so that they made dancing skeleton shadows in the moonlight. It whipped Christopher's cloak, blowing it in giant batwings, and tore through Columb's ragged jersey and breeches.

"What's that?" Christopher pointed down the road where a dark shape moved fitfully against the wind, a weaving shadow, blending with the darkness, half hidden by the shadows around it.

"It's Finn," Columb said. "Hey, Finn, you solid man!" He ran down the road toward his brother.

They walked back together, Columb's arm across his twin's shoulders.

"Has old Mick gone?" he asked.

Finn nodded. His face was pallid, freckle-blotched in the moonlight. "A couple of hours ago. I stayed till the end."

They fought their way against the wind and into the shelter of the refectory wall.

Columb faced his brother. "I'm glad you were there," he said simply. "It would ease the end for Mick."

"He starved to death, you know. He gave the food we left with him to the Brennan children, the wee ones next door."

Columb shivered. "Och, no! Sure there was no need. We could—"

"There was a need," Finn said. "Two of the Brennan children are dead."

Christopher pushed them roughly, deep into the deeper shadows.

"What is it?" They peered cautiously over the top of the broken wall into the moon-washed, shadow-jumping night.

"I don't know. I thought I saw something moving. Over there, by the west side of the abbey."

They tried to see through the changing light patterns. They tried to listen, but there was nothing to hear but the wind in the trees.

"Over there," Christopher said. "Look!"

Blackness slithered behind a swaying bush and was still. Then another shadow joined it, and another.

"And there." Columb pointed. "A hundred yards or so to the right. Behind the big rock."

Their eyes, sharpened with the watching, saw more shadows moving in and out among the swaying elms and the bare whistling whins.

"How many?" Finn breathed.

"I don't know. A dozen anyway, maybe more."

"I was followed." Finn stared at Columb and Christopher and his face was heartsick. "Saints above, they followed me."

"Come on." Christopher edged cautiously backward. "Let's get down to the others."

It was Witch who opened the door. "Finn," she said, hugging his arm, her face alive with delight. "Thanks be to this blessed day for the good that does be in it!" She looked up at his face. "What is it? What's wrong?"

"Finn was followed." Christopher bolted the door and

stood with his back against it. "They're here at the abbey."

"But how did you let yourself be followed?" Tinker's voice was thick with disgust.

"I didn't hear a thing. I looked back, but I saw nothing."

"Three could get away on the horses maybe," Christopher said.

Columb spoke quickly. "The Mullens needn't go. They know all about us and we wouldn't get far."

"Christopher, you for one should make a run for it," Finn said. "No use you getting into such trouble and this not even your country."

Christopher's eyes were steady. "Don't you think Ireland's worth a little trouble? Anyway, maybe it's time Sir James found out I'm not the milksop he takes me for. Witch, you go and take Skibbereen."

"And where would I go to?" Witch asked sharply. "You want rid of me, I suppose. You think I'd be no good in a fight. Not as good as one of your precious boyos! Well, I'm as good—besides," she went on, interrupting herself, "I don't know anybody but what's here and my six brothers in America. And I want to stay with Com."

"That leaves you, Rat—and Tinker and Roper. Go now, while there's still time."

"Not me," Rat said. "There's no sense to me going. This is the only home I've got."

"Tinker?"

The snap of Tinker's knife was sharp in the silence. "I don't run," he snarled and his teeth gleamed white in the gloom. "I stay and I fight."

"Roper?"

Roper shook his head. He slapped his rope against his legs. "I'm thinking you might need me. I can get a wheen of them if there's room to swing."

They looked at each other in silence.

"Maybe the ghosts'll save us again," Witch said.

Christopher was sniffing the air. "Don't count on it. Does anyone smell what I smell?"

Tinker's nose twitched. "Aye. That's one smell I'd know anywhere. Tinkers are afeard of that more than anything in the world."

"Well, what is it?" Witch's voice trembled. "What are you afeared of?"

"Fire," Tinker said. "That's smoke. They're going to burn us out."

18

THE BEGINNING OF THE END

"Smoke!"

"Aaragh," Witch whispered. "They're after roasting us alive."

"And what about the ghosts?" Rat said. "If they burn down the abbey, what'll the ghosts do?"

"They'll not burn down the abbey." Columb went to stand next to Witch. "Everything's too wet and the stones are too bare to catch fire. What they're going to do is smoke us out."

"They've likely started the flames with some dry hay and they've got it where the wind will catch it and blow it toward the wet grass and weeds around the abbey." Christopher's face was grim. "Sir James isn't going to venture inside these walls again, however much he wants us caught. But in a few minutes there'll be so much smoke down here we won't be able to breathe. Then we'll have to go to him."

"Quick!" Rat said. "Stuff something around the door. Fill in all the cracks."

They worked frantically, tearing pieces from their clothing and pushing the rags into the cracks and the ventilation slits high on the walls.

"The chimney!" Witch cried as smoke started billowing out of the hearth, clouding the room with a gray-black fog.

Columb grabbed the saddlebags Christopher had brought and poked them up the chimney, but that made it worse.

Great gusts belched from around the bags, filling their throats with the acrid smell of burning canvas.

Skibbereen started coughing, and Tinker took his dirty red-spotted handkerchief from the door crack, dipped it in the water bucket, and tied it around the little boy's face.

Columb had pulled the burning saddlebags from the chimney and was wafting at the smoke with the empty meal sack, trying to drive it up and out, but it was no use. It oozed in through the rags in the ventilators, around and under the door.

They were all coughing and spluttering, their eyes streaming water that made small white snail tracks down the black soot of their faces.

"It's no good," Christopher gasped. He swung Skibbereen up into his arms, unbolted the door, and ran into the passageway, the others behind. The smoke was so thick that they had to feel their way along to the steps. Half falling, choking, weeping, Christopher reached the stone slab, got it open, and was outside.

It wasn't much better out than in. The smoke was everywhere. The abbey, the cloisters, the refectory were smothered in it. The wind moved it in thick eddies, swirling it, streaking it into the cloud-driven sky.

They stood panting, breathing greedily whatever air their burning throats could find.

Rat had dragged Murphy. The man was unconscious, for the smoke had reached him before it had reached them. They were all out now, panting and retching, on their knees in the cold, black cloisters.

Columb had the horses. One of them had given him trouble, and he had pulled the empty meal sack over its head. The horses hacked harshly, their breathing like rusty bellows.

Obadiah heaved, his tongue a blackened snake that hung from his mouth.

Gradually, one by one, they crept or crawled or staggered out beyond the ring of burning, stinking weeds and smoldering grasses, outside the walls of the abbey.

"Get your hands up, all of you." The voice was hard. "Don't try to get away, for the place is surrounded."

Then another voice, cold, rich with triumph. "Got you, gentlemen, one and all."

Columb raised his eyes. Through their burning he saw the fat, squat figure on the big black stallion. Sir James!

"Sergeant Raftery. Tie them up and take them into the jail. And get that dog. Put a shot in him."

With a last ounce of strength that he didn't know he had, Columb lunged for Obadiah. "Go, fellow, go!" he croaked, hitting out at the big dog with the empty sack in his hand. "Go, I tell you!"

Obadiah blinked at him through his small, reddened eyes.

"Go, I said."

"Away from that dog, man, or this shot'll get you instead of him."

Columb struck the dog again. Obadiah whimpered and tried to lick his hand.

Suddenly, something swooped through the air and landed quivering in the dirt by the dog's paws. It was Tinker's knife.

"Get out of here, you gormless paghill," Tinker screamed, throwing himself toward the dog.

Obadiah looked at him mournfully, accusingly, and then began to run.

The sound of Sergeant Raftery's shot echoed off the abbey walls, setting the crows to cawing noisily, losing itself on the windswept bog. It had missed. Obadiah was gone, a lost shadow in the night.

"You!" Sir James pointed to Columb. "Come over here. Are you the one we followed from Ballykern?"

Columb stood silent, his body drooping with fatigue.

"Answer me when I speak to you." The riding crop came down across Columb's shoulders, fluttering the ragged remains of his shirt. "If you're wondering how we knew you were in Ballykern, I'll tell you." The oily voice was mocking. "You were given away by one of your own, a true Irishman, one of the very same you were risking your neck to help." He laughed. "I knew ten pounds would buy any Irish loyalty. I could likely have had you for two!"

"You lie." The voice was strong and loud and clear. It came from the line of soldiers a few yards behind Sir James.

Someone came out of the darkness to stand beside Columb. It was Crum.

He faced Sir James calmly. "I say you lie, Sir. He was not betrayed by an Irishman, but by one of your own servants who happened to see him in the village. An Englishman, I'm ashamed to say, adding to the ills my countrymen have already done in this poor miserable land."

Sir James's face was livid in the moonlight. "Why you—!"

"A winner can afford to be honest if not generous, Sir James, and I think we all have to admit that you are the winner." Crum's salute was as smart and quick and respectful as anyone could wish; so why, Columb wondered, did it look so insulting?

"Sergeant. Take this man and flog him. Fifty lashes, and I want to be present when the sentence is being carried out."

"Just a minute, Sir James. The law says a man can no longer be flogged without a court-martial. But then, you never did worry overly much about the law, did you?"

"Who's that?" Sir James peered through the shifting darkness at the black-faced boy with the smaller boy in his arms. The boy who had spoken.

"It's not—? Christopher!" Sir James leaned across his horse's neck to see better. "It can't be."

"Oh, but it is."

They faced each other grimly, the warmly clad gentleman on his fine black stallion and the boy, dirty, grimy, his clothing in tatters. And it was the man who looked away first.

"Take the others in," he said gruffly. "Master Christopher will stay with me."

Christopher put Skibbereen on the ground next to Witch. He moved slowly toward Sir James and raised his hand. Sir James bent to take it, a smile of triumph on his face. With one jerk Christopher had him off the horse and sprawling on the ground.

With a mammoth leap, his feet never touching the ground, Columb was in the saddle and wheeling the big stallion away from the abbey. "Thanks, Christopher!" he yelled over his shoulder. "I thank you, my friend."

He saw Sergeant Raftery's rifle come up and then he heard Sir James scream from the ground. "Don't shoot. You'll hit my horse. That stallion's worth a hundred guineas."

Then Columb heard nothing more, for he and the horse were swallowed up in the blessed, concealing smoke.

19

TRELLAGH JAIL

"This jail's as black as a tomb in Glasnevin, so it is," Witch whispered, "and as cold as Callenden. Where are you all? I can't see my foot before me."

"I'm right here." Finn's voice was loud and calm. "We're all here, excepting Com. Christopher?"

"Aye. I've got Skibbereen. I'll bring him over to you, Witch."

Witch could hear Christopher's feet slithering cautiously across the floor. "I'm this way," she said, to guide him. She felt Skibbereen's small hands moving across her hair and eyes, and then he was standing beside her with his cold face buried in her neck.

"Rat?"

"Aye."

"Roper?"

Roper's voice was muffled. "They took my rope, so they did. I don't ever mind a time when I didn't have my rope."

"And they took my knife," Tinker said.

"Well, don't spit," Witch said quickly. "You never know who's close to you and things are bad enough. Finn, where do you think Com went? Will he get us out of here?"

"I don't know how he'd do that. This place is powerful well guarded."

Rat spoke in his soft, gentle voice. "They weren't bad—the soldiers, I mean. I don't think they liked bringing us in, but I suppose they had to do what they're told."

"The one who had me across his horse wrapped his saddle blanket around me," Witch said. "And he raised my head so it didn't thump against the beast's side."

"Och, people are people, you know," Rat said, "and there's good in all of them, Irish or English."

"I keep thinking about that gormless dog." Tinker's voice was bitter. "There I had to go and throw my knife at him. I might have been able to keep it on me if they hadn't seen it. And then did you all see the way the stupid beast looked at me? Like—like I had betrayed him or something!"

"I'm thanking you for that, Tinker," Finn said. "You saved the dog all right."

"Me saving a dog! Me that hates them like poison!"

"You didn't hate Obadiah," Finn said. "You liked him, once you got to know him."

"It's like the Irish and the English." There was the suggestion of a smile in Christopher's voice. "Right, Finn?"

"Right!"

"Well, I don't know anything about that." The chittering of Witch's teeth sounded like small crickets in the darkness. "I do know we're all going to be froze stiff by the morning."

"Everybody over by Witch," Christopher said. "We'll keep each other warm."

They shuffled and crawled and felt their way in the thick blackness to the corner where Witch and Skibbereen sat.

"Brr!" Witch shivered. "Sit on top of me, somebody, for I'm cold as an icicle froze to a thatch."

They huddled together, saying little, listening to the wind howling around the barracks, blowing in icy gusts through the small, high-barred window. Listening to the clatter of the sentries' feet as they paced up and down outside their cell. Listening to their own breathing and their own thoughts, waiting for the dawn.

The night was long. Very early in the morning, while it was still dark, they heard bugles sound and then the heavy thud of boots as the soldiers assembled in the barracks yard. By first light they saw their cell for the first time. It was small, about sixteen feet square with nothing at all in it but a dirt floor and four gray-white walls. The one narrow, barred window gave the only light.

Finn prowled around, feeling the thickness of the door, pounding on the walls and the floor. He lifted Tinker on his shoulders to peer through the window and to test the strength of the iron bars set closely together in the small space.

"Outside there's two armed sentries," Tinker reported. "And there's two more on the gate."

In the middle of the morning, a big burly fellow in a stained white apron brought them each a half farl of soda bread and a cup of water. Then, one by one, they were led out of the cell down to a small washroom at the end of the passageway.

"You must think I'm gey dangerous," Witch muttered, surveying the two armed guards who walked, one on either side of her. "And you're right, I'm better nor any of those boyos any day of the week."

Around noon they had two visitors. Sir James was elegant in royal blue frock coat and breeches. His cravat was a snowy, ruffled frill around his thick, red neck and his top hat was at least two feet high. His face glowed with satisfaction.

Sergeant Raftery stood two paces behind, properly humble, properly attentive.

"Let's get a look at you." Sir James slapped his riding crop against his leg. "Mmm, you don't look like *much*, do you?"

"Stand up when his Lordship speaks to you," Sergeant Raftery boomed.

Witch and the boyos sat where they were, on the dirt floor, their backs against the cold, white wall.

"Stand up, I tell you," Raftery said again. "You scum. Didn't anybody teach you to stand in the presence of your betters?"

"I'm afraid our manners have been neglected these past years," Finn said softly. "We were too busy just staying alive. Besides, 'Evil communications corrupt good manners,' and there's been a lot of English around! The Bible," he added, at the perplexed look on Sergeant Raftery's face.

Sir James laughed. He was in such a good humor nothing was going to bother him. "Sit where you are, then. And good morning to you, Master Christopher. How did you sleep? I trust the night here has brought you to your senses and you are ready to come home with me."

Christopher raised his eyebrows. "I slept well, thank you. A clear conscience. And you? Any nightmares?"

Sir James frowned. "If I know you, another day of this'll soften you up."

Christopher smiled and nodded. "If you know me," he repeated. "Perhaps."

"I just wanted to let you know," Sir James said, "that the County Quarter Sessions are to be held this week and you'll be brought up before them. I'm sure you'll get a fair trial." He smiled, looking at them one by one. His eyes lingered on Witch. "And this is the girl, eh? Well, I suppose, a thief is a thief, whatever the sex."

Witch glared at him, her eyes hard and green as emeralds.

"Oh, aye," she said. "And a thief's a thief, whether he's stealing food for the starving people, or from them, to line his own pockets. More's the pity."

"Or from Her Majesty, the Queen," Christopher added.

Sir James's face reddened with anger. "Don't go making

accusations you can't prove. Your father may be an important man in England, but I'm the important one over here."

Witch yawned. "Oh well, as *my* father used to say, there's no use looking for justice in this world. We'll all have to wait for the next! And what about Com? Have you found him yet?" She tried to keep her voice steady.

Sir James spoke through clenched teeth. "That's none of your business. I hear from my loyal servant, Murphy, that you, miss, are the worst of the bunch!"

Witch grinned. "Well, old Murphy has more sense than I took him for. Do you hear that, the rest of you? Old Murphy says I'm the worst of the bunch!"

Sir James turned sharply toward the door of the cell. "I'll see you all at the trial. And by the way, I forgot to mention that I am the circuit judge, so you can rest assured that justice will be done." He paused. "Mm, yes, I do believe I'll break the rules just a little bit and tell you that I have already decided on your sentence. Have you heard of 'transportation'?" He smiled. "I can see you have," he said to Finn. He bowed toward Christopher. "There will, of course, be special leniency for you."

The door clanged shut behind him.

"Jakers," Tinker said into the silence. "What's the sense in having a trial at all with that ould curwheeble for the judge? Sure he has already made his mind up that we're guilty. But what is this trans—thing anyway, Finn? I've never heard of it."

"Aye, Finn, what is it?"

"Well, it's better than being hanged, I suppose, but not much," Finn said slowly. "It's what they call shipping you out of Ireland."

"To America?" Witch asked, leaning forward in excitement. "Faith and that's a punishment I'd go along with."

Finn shook his head and smiled. "It's not a reward they're after giving you, Witch! Transportation's to Australia."

Witch scratched her head. "Where in the name of all that's holy is Australia?"

"It's a big country, far away. It's where all the worst of the convicts are sent. The prisoners build roads and work in the fields and are locked up in what they call penal colonies." His voice trailed into silence.

"You mean—like jails?" Rat asked. "Forever?"

Finn nodded, his eyes carefully lowered.

"But—" Witch started. "I don't want to go to this place. I'm not going to be put out of my own country if I don't want to be going. Only if they send me to America, to Brendan and Eamonn and the rest of them. I won't go. I just won't go."

Rat covered her hand with his. "Hush, Acushla. Maybe it'll not be that bad. Even that crabbit old fellow would surely not banish us from our own dear land, not when his temper cools."

"Och," Tinker said furiously. "Sure and he would. What do you think he was looking so pleased about? He knows the thing that would hurt us the most. The softest thing about that old stick's his teeth, and they're hard and yellow as an old jackass's." He prowled up and down, from wall to wall, his mouth a tight line under the angry beak of his nose.

"What's it like, this Australia?" Rat asked.

"We'll likely never get that length," Finn said. "I mind old Mick telling me that those convict ships are as bad as coffin ships. They founder with all hands as often as they get there. It's an easy way to dispose of a problem."

"Is it far from America?" Witch wailed.

Finn nodded. "The other side of the world, Witch."

"Well, I'll never see them again, then." Witch's voice was low and desolate as the gray waters of Corrib lapping on a lonely shore. "Aaragh! They do be gone from me forever." She wrapped her arms around her chest and rocked herself back and forth in despair.

Skibbereen stroked her hair and then wormed his small, cold hand into hers.

Witch rocked and moaned. "Sorra the day, sorra the day," she keened. "Sorra the day we were born to this."

128

Tinker clenched his fists and threw back his head. "Well, you can all cry and complain, but I'm for doing something. I'll be no soft man to sit here and let them take me." He spat into the corner, but Witch no longer cared.

Roper spoke for the first time. "Will they give me back my rope?"

Christopher watched Roper's hands, curling and uncurling as though they had lives of their own. "You don't need your rope," he said. "We all just need each other."

Rat rubbed his chin. "What you're saying, Finn, is that we're to be slaves for the rest of our days."

Finn didn't answer.

Witch lifted her head and saw his face and recognized a misery as great as her own. In a few steps she was at his side, her cheek pressed against his. "Hush, hush, Acushla," she murmured. "We're not away yet."

Finn's voice was muffled. "If I have to go, I hope my brother's with me. I don't think I could bear it my lief alone, Witch. I don't think I could."

Witch closed her eyes. Where are you, Com, she thought. I can't bear it, either. I don't think I can.

20

A WILD RIDE

Columb leaned low on the horse's neck. His back cringed. He could almost feel the cold white heat of the bullet ripping into his flesh, tearing through muscle and bone. But the bullet didn't come, and with each long stride of the black stallion's powerful legs, Columb's breath eased in his throat.

I'm away, he thought exultantly. I've done it! He reined the horse to a stop and together they stood, panting, the both of them beaded with damp sweat.

Columb felt a quick rush of excitement when he realized

that he still held the precious sack, with the V.R. stamped on it in the big incriminating letters. "I've got the evidence," he muttered to himself. "Now what can I do with it?" He tried to think clearly. I've got to get to Lord Bessborough. He's the only one who can do anything for them now. Och, I wish Finn was with me. He'd know where Bessborough town is and I can't for the life of me think where it's at. He tried to remember what Christopher had said. Killarney. No, Kilkenny. Two days' ride away, or a day and a night, he thought grimly. It must be north. Almost every county in Ireland was to the north of Waterford.

He wiped his arm across his forehead and looked around. On either side the white countryside lay empty and silent, checkered with moon shadows.

He turned his horse so that he faced Waterford town on the east coast. The north must lie to his left, away from the slow-flowing river. He talked gently to the horse. "You and me have never rightly met, fellow, but we have a long way to go together. We'd better learn to like each other. I reckon after Sir James, anybody must be an improvement!"

The big black stallion snorted softly and tossed his head.

"All right," Columb said, "let's go." He leaned low across the horse's neck, digging his heels into his sides. "We're off, and we'll not be stopped till we reach Kilkenny!"

They rode through the darkness. The little villages and towns they galloped through lay sleeping, or dying, in the night. Once a scraggly red fox darted across the road in front of them, its eyes green and wild in the moonlight.

"And how did you survive?" Columb shouted after its disappearing, bushy tail. "How did you miss the stewpot?"

There was time to think as he rode, too much time. He imagined the others, lying somewhere, likely in a dark hole of a cell. Wild things, caged. He relived the fight through the smoke and the memory started his throat to burn and his eyes to water. He thought about Christopher. Christopher, in the time since he'd known him. Working through the night to unload the barge, first into the abbey on the night Witch had disappeared, caring nothing for his own safety. Christopher tonight, turning down the chance to escape. "Don't you think Ireland's worth a little trouble?" And later, speaking up for Crum, another Englishman who'd helped them.

And he thought of himself and looked at himself and didn't like what he saw. "I'm sorry, Christopher," he muttered, and knew somehow, that he was saying sorry, too, to Crum and to all Englishmen of goodwill who bore unjustly the collective hatred of Irishmen.

By dawn they had reached Mullinahone in Tipperary. Columb blinked his sore, tired eyes and peered at the two arms of the yellow signpost that marked a division of the road north of the town. One arm said "Cashel," the other "Callan." Columb scratched his head. "Well now, which will it be?" he asked the big stallion. "I've never heard tell of either of the two."

The horse wheeled quickly, strongly, to the right.

"Callan! All right. You're probably smarter than me, anyway."

Around noon they stopped at a horse trough on the roadside. The warmth of the sun had melted the ice from the top of the water and it floated in smooth, brittle sheets on the surface.

The horse drank greedily, noisily, snorting as the water burned his nose. Columb ducked his face into the brackish, brown depths, spluttering at its icy shock. He shook his head to shed the water, flinging diamond drops in all directions.

A tall thin man with hair as red as Columb's own was filling turf into a wheelbarrow in the field next to the road.

"Good day to you," Columb called. "Can you tell me, am I in the county of Kilkenny?"

The man nodded. "Aye, you do be close by Callan."

"I'm looking for the town of Bessborough. Do you know where it is?"

The man nodded again. The big Adam's apple in his thin

throat moved up and down as he spoke. "It's a fair piece away. Stay on this road to Kilkenny town. Bessborough does be over the river, maybe twenty miles from here."

"Thank you, and God save you, sir."

"Save you kindly," the man answered gravely, returning to his turfs.

Columb and the big horse rode on. They were both tiring and the stallion's stride was shorter now and slower. Columb felt light-headed. "No sleep for two nights," he reassured himself, "and only a bowl of stirabout in my belly."

The horse's black mane blowing against his face reminded him of Witch. He gritted his teeth, feeling the tightness of tension along the edge of his jaw. Witch! He remembered her prophecy the first time they had ridden together to Kildoran Abbey, when she had seen all the boyos in jail, excepting himself. He had wondered then where he came in, in the story. Now he knew. His fingers touched the coarse jute sack that he had pushed under the saddle and he urged the horse on faster and still faster.

In the late afternoon they crossed the bridge over the river Nore. The shadows were already beginning to lengthen on the road, and the wind was rising again in the bare trees.

"Not much longer now," Columb muttered, and he didn't know if he was talking to himself, or the horse, or both.

"BESSBOROUGH: 3 MILES." The words on the signpost danced crazily before his eyes and the air seemed to be filled with little black specks that floated and shimmered and hung above him. When he blinked, they disappeared.

"Come on. We're almost there." The hollowness of his voice echoed on his ears.

Bessborough was a small town, not much bigger than Ballykern. Columb had no trouble finding where the lord lieutenant lived, for his estate stretched for miles behind the tall stone wall that bordered the main road. Massive iron gates bore a coat of arms. Two gatehouses, one on either side, held a sentry, rifle in hand, standing to attention.

Columb climbed stiffly from his horse and rattled the

gate. "Please," he said, "is this the residence of Lord Bessborough?"

One of the soldiers came over to the gate. "It is. Who wants to know?"

Columb held on to the ornate iron of the gate. He felt that if he let go his legs would fold under him. "I've come a long ways. It's a matter of life and death."

The soldier laughed. His laugh echoed and rang in Columb's ears and spiraled around in the emptiness of his head. "Life and death, life and death, life and death," the soldier seemed to say, and his body had five heads and they spun in a circle close to Columb's face and then they got smaller and smaller until they disappeared into the distance.

When Columb awakened, he was in the warmth of the gatehouse. He lay on a black, slippery, shiny couch, oilcloth-covered, in front of a roaring fire. A mug of strong, sweet tea was being held to his lips.

"There now, take it easy. You'll be right as rain in a minute. Rode a long distance, did you?" The soldier's round, red face was kind and concerned. "My mate has gone up to the big house to report this to his Lordship. He'll be back presently."

Columb gulped the tea. It tasted like tar and he drank it gratefully.

"The horse." He struggled to sit up. "Where's the horse?"

"Don't worry about him. He's right outside, tied to the railing. Don't worry about him. He's a magnificent beast, so he is."

The door opened abruptly and an elderly gentleman came into the room. He was almost bald, with a soft gray fringe of hair that curled around his ears. His eyes peered short-sightedly from behind rimless glasses.

The soldier jumped to his feet and saluted, spilling the remains of the tea on Columb's breeches.

"Now, now," the elderly gentleman said absently. "I just want to talk to the boy." He looked at Columb through the round glasses. "I am Lord Bessborough. I hear you want to see me on a matter of life and death. What is it? Are you in need of food? Is your family without shelter?"

Columb stared up and into kindly blue eyes. "No, Sir. I have had the hunger, same as everyone else. And my family is dead, all save my brother, Finn. I've not come for me, but for my friends."

Lord Bessborough pulled a straight chair over by the fire and sat down. He spread his hands, palms up, in an almost humorous gesture. "I'm here. Tell me."

Columb talked for a long time.

One of the soldiers was sent out to bring the marked sack from under the saddle. Lord Bessborough turned the sack round and round in his hands and sighed heavily. He took off his glasses and rubbed his eyes. "It's hard to believe. And you tell me Lord Piddington's son has been working with you?"

"Yes, Sir. It took me a long time to trust Christopher Piddington," Columb said. "I'm ashamed of it now, for people are people, after all."

"Old hatreds die hard," the old man said. He rose slowly. "My personal secretary, Mr. Palmer, will have to handle this matter on my behalf. I am scheduled to speak in the House of Lords this week, and tomorrow I sail for England."

He put his hand on Columb's shoulder and turned to the soldiers. "When he's rested, bring him up to the house for the night. I will see you in the morning before you leave," he told Columb.

21

IN THE BARRACKS YARD

The dark of another night was falling, their third in Trellagh jail. The cell was cold with a coldness that was partly physical and partly the cold of despair.

Witch was the first to hear the commotion outside. At first she thought it was a part of the noise of the big army barracks. "Would you listen to them!" she said. "Sure they must be the heaviest-footed craters in the world!"

Then the loud, hollow thumping began and the noise rose and swelled till it roared like a risen torrent.

They all stood up, looking at each other excitedly.

"Tinker, climb on my shoulders and see what's going on," Finn said.

"Jakers!" Tinker pressed his face against the bars. "There's a mob of people outside the big gate, and they're trying to knock it down."

"Is it Com?" Witch asked eagerly. "I'll bet my old boots it's Com, come to save us."

Tinker shook his head so his gold earring flashed in the lamplight from the barracks yard. His face was shadow-striped. "I don't see Com, but it looks like the half of the people from Trellagh and Ballykern and Magheragh too. Listen!"

They could hear the chant that came, beating with the banging on the gate.

"Let the boyos go! Free the Boys from Waterford! Let the boyos go!"

Witch started a jig, swinging Skibbereen till his head lolled loosely on his neck. "We're saved, we're saved. We'll never be sent to Australia. We'll never be sent to Australia."

Skibbereen laughed aloud.

"Don't be too sure." Tinker spoke from his perch at the window.

Outside, a bugle sounded and feet clattered on the hard ground.

"Every soldier in the barracks is out in the yard. Raftery's lining them up in front of the gates and they have a stand of arms."

Witch tugged at his legs. "Get down, Tinker. I want to see."
They changed places.

"The gate's going to give any minute," Witch breathed.

"Oh Finn, do you think Com's leading them? I don't see him at all at all."

With a heavy thud the barred wooden gate fell inward and the mob surged through into the barracks yards.

"Let the boyos go! Let the boyos go!"

Armed with shillelaghs and old rusty pitchforks and spades that hadn't turned a potato in months, they poured forward, their faces tense and grim.

"Oh, they're marvelous altogether, so they are," Witch said softly. "They haven't an ounce of strength between them, but their hearts are as big as barrels!" She blinked her eyes. "Listen. Sergeant Raftery's reading them the Riot Act, but they're paying him no heed." She saw a child stumble and fall and a thin, scraggy man in a stovepipe hat pick her up without breaking his stride. Then there was a loud fusillade and a sudden silence.

"Get back, you people. That round was over your heads. The next will be amongst you."

Every word came clearly into the small bleak cell, filling it with horror.

Witch pressed her mouth against the bars. "Go back!" she shouted. "Don't get yourselves killed."

A man stepped out from the crowd. In the clear yellow lamplight, his face was the face of an old, old man, but his voice when he spoke was clear and strong and youthful.

"We ask a word with you, sergeant. We have something to say."

Sergeant Raftery moved toward them and even his walk was angry.

"You have nothing to say that I want to listen to. If I had the room I'd put the lot of you rabble-raisers in there with the others."

"Sir," the man said in his ringing voice. "These are but children you have locked away. Children who were forced to grow up too soon. Let them go. They saved our lives. For the sake of the future between our country and England, free them now. As a gesture of goodwill that will be known throughout the land. We have asked for little from England and gotten less. Now we ask for this. The release of the boyos and the girl."

Sergeant Raftery raised his gun. "On the count of three, I fire."

Witch watched in horror as men pushed women and children behind them and stood their ground.

"You may fire then," the man said. " 'Twill not be the first massacre on Irish soil, or the last."

"One—two—"

"Just a minute, sergeant. What's going on here?"

Witch rubbed the top of Finn's head gleefully. "Oh, musha this day," she whispered. "It's two fine gentlemen riding handsome horses. They're coming through the gap where the gate used to be and you can see from here they're powerful angry. They're saying something to Raftery." Witch squeezed her ears to the bars, but there was no need, for the man's voice sounded clearly in the small cell.

"I can't believe my eyes! Would you have shot these people?" The man's voice was cold and fierce. He towered a good six inches over Raftery's head. He turned and faced the crowd. "I am Henry John Johnson. You know of me. I have come to the County of Waterford to help feed your people. There will be soup kitchens here in a week. I hear tell you have enough to last you till then, and I hear tell that those inside are the ones responsible for keeping you alive. Go home now. I promise you I will talk to the sergeant, and if it is within my power to help these boyos, I will."

"Did you hear that?" Witch craned her neck to see farther. "It's Henry John Johnson himself. Now they're all moving inside, the two men and the sergeant, and the soldiers are breaking ranks."

She clambered down from Finn's shoulders. "What do you think, Finn? Will he be able to help us?"

"I don't know, Witch. I just don't know. We'll have to wait and see."

They had about a quarter of an hour to wait. Feet came

quickly along the passageway and the door was unbolted and flung open. Two gentlemen entered the cell, Sergeant Raftery walking silently behind them. He held a lantern and its soft yellow light threw long shadows across the bare floor of the cell and up the cold, white walls.

"Bring that lamp closer, sergeant. I can't see a thing. Do you mean to say they're not even allowed a light in here? And it's unbearably cold." The man shivered, huddling his cloak about him. Behind him, Raftery muttered something about "orders," but the man paid no attention.

"Here, give me the lamp," he said impatiently. "Mr. Simpson. You keep your eyes open. We want to be accurate about what we saw here."

The boyos moved forward into the circle of lamplight, but Witch sat where she was, in the corner by the far wall. Skibbereen dozed in her lap.

Christopher held out his hand. "I'm happy to meet you, sir. I am Christopher Piddington, these are my friends. Finn Mullen, Tinker, Rat, and Roper. The girl over there is Miss Ryan O'Callahan, and the little one is Skibbereen."

The man shook his hand. "Henry John Johnson, and this is Alistair Simpson. But you," he said, still gripping Christopher's hand, "if I'm not mistaken, you're English!"

Christopher grinned. "I am, sir. But it's not something I've been overly proud of this past year."

Henry John Johnson nodded his head. "How did you get involved in this?"

"It's a long story. You'll have to hear it another time."

"Yes," Henry John Johnson said. "Tonight, without delay, Alistair and I will ride to Blunt Manor and plead your case to Sir James. I feel sure when he knows the reasons for your actions he'll let you go with a reprimand."

Finn and Christopher exchanged glances. "I think not, sir. I feel it will not be quite that simple."

"But surely, these were his tenants. They were his responsibility. I met him once. He seems a pleasant fellow, with the welfare of his people at heart."

"Och musha, sir," Witch said from her shadowy corner. "You wouldn't believe a thing that fellow swore on a pile of holy books. Sure he wears as many coats as an onion and changes them to suit his company."

"But," Henry John Johnson said, less surely, "he told me that he issued free grain when he had it and that he had let rents go unpaid since times got so hard."

Witch snorted. "Begob and he ties knots with his tongue teeth couldn't unravel!" She shook her head. "As you would say, sir, the truth does not be in him." She eased the weight of Skibbereen in her arms. "Do you—do you think you gentlemen will be able to help us? We're well used to looking after ourselves this past wee while, but being locked away makes it hard, so it does."

"We'll do our best," Henry John Johnson said. But there wasn't enough strength in the words to kindle the heat of hope in any of them.

22

FIVE INCHES
IN FIVE MINUTES

"Absolutely not!" Sir James adjusted his black cravat and inspected himself in the mirror. Behind him, Henry John Johnson stood, hat in hand.

Sir James turned to face him. "They broke the law and they will suffer for it. And what is worse, they defied me and turned my people against me. Against me, their benefactor for twenty years."

"I have always found the Irish to be a simple people," Henry John Johnson said, "but not stupid. It's difficult to believe that if you have been a good landlord all these years they would turn against you for no reason."

The color deepened in Sir James's face. "Believe what you like." He pulled the golden bell rope that dangled by the fireplace. "If you want to know what those—those thieving scoundrels did, you're welcome to come and sit in my court today. There'll be plenty of evidence against them, I promise you."

"And what counsel has been provided for them?"

"It is a closed court. The evidence is all there."

The door opened quietly, and Murphy, dignified in black frock coat and trousers, bowed to Sir James. "Yes, your Lordship?"

"Ah yes, Murphy. Have the carriage brought to the front. You will ride with me." He turned to Henry John Johnson, his small, cold eyes hard with anger. "This man, sir, will be one of the witnesses against these rascals today. They captured him while he was trying to do his duty toward me and kept him for ten days without food or drink, in the vilest of circumstances."

"I congratulate you," Henry John Johnson said. "To have been ten days without food or drink you look remarkably well."

"And then one of them, the girl as I understand it, hit him a vicious blow over the head, for no reason whatsoever. It's a miracle he's still alive. But he is, and anxious to testify against them."

Murphy's eyes glittered. "Aye. They'll be sorry they took me from the abbey when you set it alight. It would have been better for them if they'd left me there."

Henry John Johnson spoke gently. "So one of them saved you, did he? I can see they're a wicked lot, to be sure."

"Come to the courthouse at noon," Sir James said, "and you'll hear all about it."

"I warn you, Sir James. You have not heard the last of this. I may be too late to do anything for these children, but there will be an inquiry, and you will not come out of it well."

"Really?" Sir James smoothed on a glove. "I doubt that. England holds no warm feelings for Ireland, especially now. Here!" He picked up a copy of *The Times* that lay on a side table. "Look at this."

On the front page a cartoon depicted a brutal-looking Irish laborer, one hand held out in a begging gesture, the other behind his back holding a blunderbuss.

"That's what the English think of the Irish. You'll have trouble telling them otherwise. As for this lot, I don't know anybody who'd lift a hand to save them." He picked up his hat and cane. "Come, Murphy!" He bowed briefly to Henry John Johnson. "Sir, I look forward to seeing you in court."

Witch and the boyos finished the small soda farl the guard brought them and waited for whatever was to happen next.

"I'm that nervous my stomach's going in and out like Sean O'Sullivan's old melodium at an Easter ceilidh," Witch groaned. She wiped crumbs from Skibbereen's chin.

Christopher paced the floor of the small cell, six paces one way, six the other.

"Stop walking, Christopher, will you? You're making it worse. Do you think Henry John Johnson did any good with Sir James? I wouldn't even mind if he locked us up here for a year or two, but the very thoughts of that Australia place make my heart quake."

"I wonder where Com is?" Finn mused. "It seems powerful strange to be facing this without him."

I wonder where Com is? I wonder where Com is? The words circled and recircled in Witch's mind.

Rat flattened his white hair with the palms of his hands. "It's important to look neat," he said seriously. "If you look right, people believe in you more. Maybe I should keep my eyes shut. These queer eyes of mine always get me in trouble. People think if your eyes are strange, you're strange. That's the way they reason."

"Och, Rat," Witch said. "Sure anybody with a bit of wit would know you're the softest, sweetest creature that ever breathed. What has the color of your eyes to do with it?"

Rat shrugged. "I don't know. That's the way it's always been."

"Now *everybody's* afeared of me," Tinker said. He

straightened his dirty, spotted handkerchief and gathered himself to spit.

"Aye," Witch said dryly. "They're afeared you'll spit in their eye when they're not looking. Roper! Stand up and let's have a look at you."

Roper shuffled to his feet, his eyes downcast, his hands moving nervously at his side.

"You know," Witch said, "I think you've shrunk since you lost your rope. Why's that?"

Roper shrugged his shoulders. "I'm nothing without my rope. Nothing at all."

"Now that's a lot of balderdash," Witch said. "Whoever told you that? If you ask me—"

They all stiffened, listening to the heavy boots coming along the passageway.

"Och, they're coming for us, so they are," Witch whispered. She put her arms around Skibbereen and held him tight.

"Top of the morning, top of the morning," Sergeant Raftery's voice boomed. His waxed mustaches gleamed like silk in the pale sunlight. He was dressed in full regalia. Scarlet coat and breeches, black cap and boots, long white gauntlets. He slapped a black riding crop against his boot and whistled tonelessly. Then he strolled into the cell and walked slowly around them all, back and front, eyeing them contemptuously.

"Whew," he said, wrinkling his nose. "You stink! I always heard the Irish were a dirty lot." He picked up a piece of Witch's long black hair with the end of his riding crop, shuddered, and dropped it quickly. "A dirty female's worse than a dirty cow. The cow only rolls in its own clap."

With one leap Roper flung himself on Raftery's back. He twined his short, wiry legs around the sergeant's waist and his arms around his neck, sinking his teeth into the red roll of fat that rose above Raftery's stiff black collar.

"Get off of me, you scum," Raftery bellowed, slapping his crop awkwardly behind him at Roper's back.

"Tell Witch you're sorry," Roper grunted, removing his teeth for as long as it took to say the words and then biting again, more deeply than before.

"Ow, ow—get off of me!"

Roper clung, leechlike, his teeth hidden in the flesh of Raftery's neck. "Tell her!"

"Don't talk with your mouth full, Roper, it isn't polite," Christopher said.

Suddenly Skibbereen laughed and clapped his hands.

"Did you hear that, Roper?" Witch called. "Even the wee one's cheering you on!"

"Bailey! McKee! Get in here!" Raftery yelled.

"Tell her," Roper said.

Witch was grinning. Her teeth, white and shining and pointed as a vixen's, snapped viciously as though she too could taste Raftery's flesh.

Bailey and McKee came at a run. Their eyes widened at the sight of Raftery carrying Roper on his back.

"Tell her!"

"Ow, ouch, get him off!"

The two soldiers untangled Roper's arms and legs but his teeth held fast. They seemed locked, like a rabid animal's, in Raftery's neck. The soldiers beat Roper about the head and face with their fists, but he held on, eyes tightly closed, his face as scarlet as Raftery's jacket.

"I didn't mean it. I'm sorry, girl, I'm sorry."

Roper unclenched his teeth and slithered to the ground where he lay panting, the veins in his neck thick as bootlaces.

Raftery rubbed at the marks Roper's teeth had left on his pink skin. His eyes blazed hatred. He lifted his polished black boot and kicked Roper in the stomach.

Roper doubled up, his arms about his body.

Tinker stepped forward quickly with his arm raised to strike but Finn stopped him. "Leave them be, Tinker," he whispered. "Just leave them alone."

Raftery raised his foot again, aiming his second kick, but Witch was in the way. She shielded Roper's body with hers. "You touch him again and I'll put the Curse of Cromwell on you, Raftery. Aye, and on your sons and on your sons' sons after them. You're an Irishman, Raftery, for all your heathen ways, and never mind denying it. I'll put the curse on you till the day you die!" Her voice carried such conviction that Raftery stopped, his foot in midair.

Witch lifted Roper's head. Ignoring Raftery completely, she brushed Roper's spiky black hair from his face. "Ochone, Ochone," she whispered. "Sure you did well by me, as well as any of my own brothers, and you without your rope!" She put her arms under his shoulders. "Can you get to your feet? Here, take aholt on me."

Roper dragged himself slowly upright, his face pale but triumphant.

"Why!" Witch said in amazement. "I can't understand it at all at all. It looks to me like you've growed five inches in the last five minutes." She grinned and held out her hand and Roper took it.

He smiled down at Skibbereen who stood with his thumb in his mouth. "Give me a sup of water, somebody," he said. "There's a gey bad taste on my tongue."

Raftery brushed off his smart tunic and set his cap straight on his head. Witch looked him up and down distastefully. "Faith," she said, "and a man on a galloping horse would take you for a gentleman in that getup, if he didn't look too close."

Raftery controlled himself with an effort. "Enjoy yourselves. We'll see who has the last laugh. I can wait."

Bailey and McKee herded Witch and the boyos together and pushed them ahead into the barracks yard where an armed escort waited. Then they were marched, two by two, along the main street of Trellagh to the courthouse.

Silent people lined the street. Sad-eyed women in threadbare shawls stretched their hands in blessing as they passed. Men stood, bareheaded, their faces bleak and sorrowing.

When the courthouse gates clanged shut behind them a sigh rose from a hundred throats. It rose and swelled, a melancholy, mournful dirge. And it was as though the sound came from the heart of a doomed and dying land.

23

LAW AND JUSTICE

The courthouse was a two-storied, whitewashed building set back from the main street. The two heavy wooden doors were opened to let the prisoners in and closed again behind them. Under Sir James's orders, this was to be a closed court. A guard had been placed outside to assure that there would be no unwanted visitors.

Witch and the boyos were led by a bailiff in a dingy black suit to an enclosed wooden bench at the front of the room. Except for two soldiers inside the main doors and two at the rear doors, the bailiff and the clerk of the court, the big room was empty. Sergeant Raftery took the bench behind them.

In a few minutes the rear doors opened and Henry John Johnson and Alistair Simpson entered. They came straight across to Witch and the boyos.

"We just drove here with Sir James in his carriage." Johnson's face was bleak as he looked at the flicker of hope in their eyes. He shook his head. "He won't listen to anything I say. He's determined that you'll all suffer."

Christopher slammed his fist against the wooden bench. "He can't send them away. He just can't!"

Henry John Johnson spoke quietly. "I don't know when the next convict ship leaves for Australia, but I know they're going fairly frequently, now that the worst of the winter's over. He'll probably order you taken to Spike Island right away to wait for transportation there."

"Where's Spike Island?" Witch wet her dry lips with the tip of her tongue.

"It's off the Cove of Cork. It's the convict depot." Witch shuddered and Skibbereen pushed his small hand into hers.

"Listen," Christopher said desperately. "We've got to get

word to my father. He may be home by now. Can you reach him? It's Dolby, in Somerset."

"We'll leave immediately the trial ends and get the packet to Bristol. But it'll take more than a week, if he is home, to get to him and get back here."

"What about in Ireland? There must be someone who can help them," Alistair Simpson said angrily. "Sir James Blunt can't be the most important man in the country."

"There's Lord Bessborough," Finn said. "He's lord lieutenant of all Ireland."

"I know he's scheduled to make a speech in the House of Lords tomorrow," Henry John Johnson said, "for it was written up in *The Times*. He must be already in England. Everything is going to depend on how quickly Sir James can get you on a ship. If there's time, we'll move heaven and earth to get you at least a fair trial."

The two men shook hands with each one of them before they took their seats.

In a few minutes Murphy entered by the rear door and sat to the left of the judge's bench. He cocked his head at the boyos and smiled, and then bowed to Witch. He crossed his legs comfortably and waited.

The four soldiers who had escorted the barge on the night of the robbery arrived next and sat behind Murphy. Crum obviously was not to testify.

The clerk of the court rapped with his gavel on the wooden table.

"Pray silence for the Honorable Sir James Blunt, Justice of the Peace, Circuit Judge of the District of Trellagh," he intoned. "Will all here please stand."

There was a shuffle of feet as the court rose.

Sir James walked to his bench and seated himself. In his black robes and curled white wig he looked like everyone's idea of law and justice.

The clerk rapped again. "The Spring Quarter Sessions of the District of Trellagh are now in session. You may be seated."

Sir James peered over the top of his desk. "Ah, yes, I know this case well." He shuffled papers in front of him and then read off their names.

"Will the prisoners please stand. You are charged with stealing an undetermined amount of food, the property of Sir James Blunt, Esquire, of the town of Ballykern in the County of Waterford, Ireland, to the approximate value of one hundred fifty English pounds. You are further charged with assault upon various members of Her Majesty's First Royal Dragoons, this violence having occurred during the perpetration of said robbery. You are also charged with kidnapping and holding against his will and by force one Seamus Cervais Murphy, servant to the aforementioned Sir James Blunt. How do you plead? Guilty or not guilty?"

Finn's voice was loud and clear. "We plead guilty, for we did all those things, but, your Lordship, we ask that you consider the circumstances under which we acted. We robbed only to feed the starving people of this townland. Any of them would be willing to testify on our behalf."

"Silence!" Sir James's gavel rang like a pistol shot in the almost empty room. "You will answer only the questions put to you. I want no speeches in my court." His voice dropped again and he smiled. "The fact that you have pleaded guilty simplifies matters. There will now be no need to call the witnesses present, so we will continue with the affairs of this court and pronounce sentence upon you without further delay.

"Christopher Piddington, please step forward. It grieves me deeply that I should have you before me in such circumstances." Sir James frowned at the papers in front of him. "However, I have taken into consideration the fact that you are very young and that you have been involved in something you did not truly understand. Therefore, having given the matter a great deal of thought, I have decided that the three days you spent in Trellagh jail are sufficient punishment for you. I shall see to it that you are sent back to England without delay and I shall inform your father that it would be best, in future, that you stay there."

147

He thumped with his gavel on the desk. "The case against Christopher Piddington is dismissed. You are free to leave this courtroom."

Christopher stood still, his head high, his eyes fixed on Sir James. "I accept the dismissal of the charges against me only because I want to be free to fight for these others, my friends." His voice was hard. "And I will fight, Sir James. Make no mistake about that. I may be young, but I understand more than you think."

"Do not tempt me by your insolence to reverse my decision," Sir James said. "Bailiffs! Take this boy outside and see that he does not reenter this court." He cleared his throat. "Now as for the rest of you." He looked with contempt at the six ragged figures standing before him. "You are to be transported to the penal colonies in Australia, there to serve a sentence of fourteen years. Ireland can do without thievery and violence, and I aim to see that there are five less scoundrels on this island."

Witch uttered a little moan and slumped back onto the bench, covering her face with her hands. Skibbereen stroked her shoulder. Tears fell from his eyes and hung glittering like jewels in the darkness of her hair.

"Stand up," Sir James said. "I have not finished yet."

Behind them, Sergeant Raftery shuffled his feet and cleared his throat.

From his seat at the side, Murphy grinned and craned his neck for a better view.

"I am not an unkind man," Sir James went on, "and I realize that waiting for a sentence to be carried out is often the hardest part. So I have ascertained that the brig *Absolute* is sailing for Australia from Spike Island the day after tomorrow. There is room aboard for the six of you. You will be on it." He stopped and wiped his mouth delicately with a snowy white handkerchief. "And the other one, the twin, we have picked up his trail. With any luck we'll have him too."

He smiled, gently, at their stricken faces.

Henry John Johnson rose to his feet. "Sir, I protest this

sentence and the haste with which it is being executed. I beg of you to remember the ages of these young people. One is only an infant. The eldest are fifteen, and I understand the girl is but fourteen. This sentence is unnecessarily harsh, indeed it is unjust. If I can make arrangements—"

"Unjust?" Sir James raised his eyebrows. "As to your arrangements, sir, I would advise you to forget them. I am the judge of this court. You are a stranger to our province and know nothing of the matter. This court is now closed. The prisoners will be returned to their jail cells and will be taken tonight to Dublin and from there to Spike Island."

Behind them Sergeant Raftery sighed contentedly.

"Bailiffs—return the prisoners—" His words were shocked into silence.

The two guards inside the front entrance had been thrown unceremoniously off balance as the heavy doors swung open.

"Just a minute!" The voice was loud and angry, and unmistakably Irish. The man who spoke was young and tall and obviously a gentleman. "Sir James Blunt?" he asked, walking toward the bench.

"What the—?"

"I am John Palmer, personal secretary to Lord Bessborough, lord lieutenant of Ireland. I bear a letter from him, addressed to you."

Sir James hesitated, frowning, and then held out his hand. He opened the letter slowly, took his eyeglasses from their case again, and put them on. His face blanched.

Mr. Palmer spoke over his shoulder. "Let the boy come in," he said impatiently. "I told you, he's with me."

"Com!" Witch was out of her seat and running up the aisle. "Oh, Com," she sobbed, throwing her arms around him, tears streaming down her face. "Com, Com."

Behind her, Finn walked, dazed, toward his brother.

"Bailiffs!" Sir James shouted. "Those are sentenced prisoners. Take them back to their seats, and the other boy too. He is one of them."

Mr. Palmer's voice was cold. "Yes. Let us all be seated, including you, Sir James."

Witch was hanging on Columb's arm, her face flushed and her eyes fever-bright. "Look at you," she whispered. "All dressed up like a dog's dinner! I hardly recognized you."

Columb glanced down at his rich brown coat and breeches and grinned sheepishly. "Aye. His lordship had them give me new clothes. My other ones didn't look too good, or smell too good, either."

"But what happened, and how did you find him, and how did you get him to send help?" Finn asked.

"It's a long story. I'll tell you later."

Skibbereen, unnoticed, ran to Columb and was swung up in his arms. His lips moved, forming words that went unsaid.

Sir James was talking. Mr. Palmer listened, nodding his head. Henry John Johnson had come to stand beside him, and he was listening too.

Sir James's eyes bulged with anger and his voice got louder by the minute. "But I tell you, they stole from me. They're guilty. They admit it themselves."

"Guilty of what?" Mr. Palmer asked. "Guilty of giving the people back their own food?"

"Guilty of keeping them alive?" Henry John Johnson asked. "For they would surely have been dead, in their hundreds, by now."

"I have been making inquiries on Lord Bessborough's behalf on the way down here, and I understand that you asked the impossible of these people. That you allowed them to die. That you helped them to die." There was added horror to the death words spoken in John Palmer's matter-of-fact voice.

"I did no such thing." Two scarlet spots glowed on Sir James's cheeks.

"We shall see," Mr. Palmer said. "I heard Lord Bessborough tell Lord John Russell just last week that the only long-term solution to the Irish problem is to rid the country of un-scrupulous landlords who bleed the people to add to their own riches." His eyes narrowed. "Lord John Russell agreed with him."

"Who in the name of Kathleen ni Houlihan is Lord John Russell?" Witch whispered gleefully to Finn. "He's a great fellow, whoever he is."

"Musha, you ignorant girl," Finn said. "He's just the prime minister of England, that's all. He's a Whig."

"I'd best not ask what a Whig is," Witch muttered to Columb, "or I'll be told I'm stupid altogether. You'd best watch your words with me, you boyos. You all know rightly I'm smarter nor any of you."

"I understand there is also a small matter of supplies stolen from Her Majesty, the Queen," Mr. Palmer was saying. "And don't tell me there's been a mistake, for we have evidence to the contrary."

Sir James came down the steps from his desk. His wig was slightly askew, giving him a rakish appearance that didn't match the fear in his eyes.

"Who is this man?" Mr. Palmer asked, pointing to Murphy, who was trying to look small in the corner of his seat.

"This is a witness against the prisoners. He came here to testify."

Murphy leapt to his feet and moved lightly toward Mr. Palmer. "Indeed, dear sir, it is an honor to meet you. I have great respect and admiration for Lord Bessborough. It is true, I did come here today to testify on behalf of these poor children. I stumbled upon them, unawares as you might say, but indeed they treated me well. They're a fine group of young people, so they are, and a credit to their country."

Sir James looked as though he might have a seizure.

Witch tittered. "Och, Murphy! You should get a look at yourself, girning and gawping like a pampered mongrel. I tell you, Murphy, the stage lost a gey bargain when they missed you."

Murphy smiled happily. "Ah, Miss Witch. You were always kindness itself to me. Kindness itself!"

Mr. Palmer looked in bewilderment from one face to the other. "We must discuss all of this later, at greater length. Sir James, according to the instructions given you in Lord Bessborough's letter, these young people are now free. Am I not right?"

Sir James nodded. "Aye," he said. "For the time being. But there'll be more about this before it's finished."

Mr. Palmer smiled. "I'm sure you're right, Sir James. I have no doubt of that whatsoever. Now, is there a place where you can all spend the night? Do you have relatives you can go to?"

Henry John Johnson stepped forward. "I would be proud to have them with me."

"We could go back to the abbey," Rat said gently. "We could clean it up."

"Aye," Tinker said. "It was good in the abbey."

"Kildoran Abbey," Columb explained. "It's outside of Ballykern, about six miles from the village. It's ruined, but there's an underground room where we've been living. I told Lord Bessborough about it." He turned to Henry John Johnson. "I thank you, sir, for your kindness in offering to have us with you. But it will be fitting that we go back to the abbey."

"Bailiff!" Mr. Palmer called. "Bring them horses. And food to take with them."

Christopher appeared in the doorway. "And bring an extra horse for me, bailiff," he said. He moved to shake hands with Mr. Palmer.

"You must be Lord Piddington's son," Mr. Palmer said. "I have met your father. Columb told me about you."

"And what did he tell you?" Christopher asked.

"That you were a true friend to Ireland and a true friend to us," Columb said. "Though there was one among us stubborn and stupid as a jackass."

Christopher grinned. "I'll not be arguing with you on that." His fake Irish accent was as bad as ever, but Columb didn't mind. He didn't mind at all.

Mr. Palmer looked puzzled, sensing something he couldn't understand. "I'm glad you came to Lord Bessborough," he said to Columb. "It's hard for him to know when something needs remedying when it all looks right on the surface."

Columb nodded. "I know, sir. But it's hard, too, for us to understand that there can be justice if we look for it. Maybe we've made a start."

Mr. Palmer smiled. "Maybe we have, Columb Mullen. Maybe we have."

The horses were waiting for them. Columb took Skibbereen in front of him and they rode, all of them, down the main street that was still lined with people. Someone started the shout, "God save the boyos," and the crowd took it up and roared it with one voice.

And the boyos knew that their freedom was not theirs alone but freedom for the people, the promise of freedom for Ireland itself.

24

THE CEILIDH

They were preparing for the ceilidh, as Irish a party as a party could be. The underground room had been swept and wiped clean of soot and now it was warm with golden furze and whin, and garlanded with boughs of evergreens. Tinker sat with his back to the wall, playing a mournful tune on his mouth organ.

"I wisht you'd play something livelier," Witch complained. "This is a celebration we're having, not a wake." She tucked a sprig of yellow whin behind her ear. "Whist, I think I hear them."

The rattle of horses and carts came clearly on the still night air.

Witch smoothed the skirt of her new red plaid dress and

took a deep breath. "Roper," she said shakily. "I'm that nervous I could kittle a quilt! Being in charge of a ceilidh is a big responsibility."

"Anybody home?" a voice called.

It was Columb who opened the door to Henry John Johnson and Alistair Simpson.

Witch took the jug of buttermilk that Simpson offered and set it on the table. She held out her hand to him. "You're welcome to the ceilidh," she said. "And you too, sir," she added to Henry John Johnson. "Draw up to the warm. There's a chill air outside."

Other footsteps clattered on the stairs and Christopher appeared in the doorway. Behind him, a tall gray-haired man with bushy sideburns looked around in amazement.

"God bless all here," Christopher said. "Witch, this is my father. Father, this is Witch, and these are the boyos."

Witch bobbed a curtsy. "Sir, we're pleased you could come. We're beholden to you, all of us, for your generosity. I thank you from the bottom of my heart. It has always been my dream to go to America and now you have made it possible."

Christopher's father smiled. "It was my pleasure, child. And you sail tomorrow?"

"Aye, with the tide. Com and Finn will take us in the cart to Waterford town."

"And you are sure that this is what you want?"

"It is, Sir. My own brothers are there, and I will keep house for them. But someday we'll be back, my brothers and me. If you're born here, Sir, you do come back before you die. That's the way it is, if you're Irish." Her hand dropped to Skibbereen's shoulder and she turned to face Henry John Johnson. "We thank you too, sir, for what you did for Skibbereen. Sure it was a brainwave to speak to Mrs. Brennan about him. He needs a mother, so he does, and Mrs. Brennan has a heart as big as Connemara. And a loneliness in it now that she's lost two of her own dear weans."

Henry John Johnson nodded. "We journeyed to the town of

Skibbereen to see if the child came from there and could go back. But if he did, nobody knows about him." His voice was low. "There are only a few left alive in the town anyway. It came close to being wiped out entirely in the famine."

"Skibbereen," Skibbereen whispered, and Witch let her hand move up to fondle his neck. "Hush, darlin'," she whispered. "Sure you'll have all those brothers and sisters from now on. You'll be talking again, saying all the words and learning more, forgetting all the bad things you saw that belong in the past." She blinked. "And I'll be thinking of you playing in the streets of Ballykern, and you trundling a hoop or playing taws." She stopped and smiled shakily. "But sure, it's America for me."

"Yes," Lord Piddington said gently. "And you, Rat? You go too?"

"Aye, We go together, the four of us. Roper and Tinker to Boston, Witch and me to New York."

"And you? Will you be back?" Lord Piddington asked.

"I never thought I'd ever go," Rat said. "But things are changing here, and we none of us has anybody left in Ireland. There's work in America, and a chance for people who have nothing."

Finn spoke softly, but they all heard.

> *"Give me your tired, your poor,*
> *Your huddled masses yearning to breathe free,*
> *The wretched refuse of your teeming shore."*

"Faith and they're the most beautiful words I ever heard in my life," Witch said. "Brendan wrote and told me. They're printed on a statue, right there in the harbor for the whole world to see." She gripped Com's arm. "Och, Com. Come with us, you and Finn and Skibbereen. We'll all go together."

Columb smiled down at her. "Skibbereen will be better here. And Finn and I, well, we've made our decision. It wasn't an easy one."

"We're staying," Finn said. "And when you come back to

visit the old country, sure here we'll be, the grandest men in all Munster."

Witch laughed, but her eyes were suspiciously bright. "Oh, aye, you'll be that, all right, if they don't hang you first."

"Where will you live?" Lord Piddington asked. "Christopher told me your cottage had been tumbled by Sir James."

"We have another home now," Finn said. "That's one of the reasons we wanted to stay. Old Mick, he was a friend of ours in Ballykern, he left us his cottage when he died. It's freehold and it's ours, along with all of his books and his big brass bed."

"We'll live there," Columb added. "Skibbereen will be next door to us and Obadiah will come back too, for he'll know. And we'll teach the children of Ballykern, the way old Mick taught us. Irish history and legend, and where all the less important countries are in the world," he added with a grin. "Even Australia!"

"And your great English writers as well as the Irish ones," Finn said. "And the Gaelic, so they'll know their own tongue, though it does be dying out in the land."

"And we'll teach them not to hate," Columb said softly. He looked at Christopher then. Their eyes met and there was no need of words between them.

"And we'll tell them about the Englishmen who helped us, when we were just boys, back in 1847 in the days of the great famine." Finn's voice was light, but there was a depth to it that they all understood.

"Speaking about Englishmen who helped us," Witch asked. "Is there any word about Crum?"

Lord Piddington smiled. "You can call him Sergeant Crum from now on. Lord Bessborough's recommendation. And you can call Sergeant Raftery just plain Raftery. He's been reduced to the ranks and transferred to the North of England."

Witch sniffed. "Just the place for him. Oh, begging you English gentlemen's pardon!"

156

"He may see his old friend Sir James Blunt there," Lord Piddington added. "I understand he's been relieved of all his land holdings in Ireland. The government felt he, er, misused his authority."

Witch clapped her hands. "Begob and my father was wrong! There is justice in this world, after all. You just have to wait on it. So poor old Murphy's lost his good job?"

Lord Piddington nodded. "I knew you'd be sad about that. He wanted to go to England with Sir James, but Sir James wouldn't have him. Something to do with his being untrustworthy. And, of course, Sir James may not be around long. There's an investigation afoot over the matter of stolen government supplies. But I understand Murphy was terribly upset at not going along. He was completely devoted to Sir James."

Witch wrinkled her nose. "Well, everyone to his own taste, as the old lady said when she kissed the cow! Now, how about food? I've made stew here that would put muscles on a cockle." She filled the earthen bowls brimful and poured thick mugs of creamy buttermilk.

They linked arms and toasted one another's health.

"May your bread ever be hot from the griddle!"

"May your meal barrel never run empty!"

"May you always have buttermilk to sup with your praties."

The ceilidh lasted till early dawn.

Tinker played "The Wearing of the Green," and "The Fisherman's Lament," and "The Kerry Dancers," and they sang and danced and told story after story till the pale sunlight slanted through the high slits in the ceiling. And then, suddenly, the gaiety died away.

"This is the day," Columb said. "The day you leave Holy Ireland."

"Aye," Tinker growled, "but we'll be back when we've made our fortunes."

"It's time we left." Lord Piddington pushed his chair back. "You have few enough hours to rest before your journey."

"One more song," Christopher said. "We'll sing 'Dark Rosaleen,' the song of the country itself."

They joined hands around the crumbling turf fire and sang the words.

"Good-bye," Christopher said. There was a roughness in his voice.

"Good-bye. Good-bye."

"We'll leave you here," Columb said, stopping the cart a few yards from the dock.

The two masts of the Sailing vessel *Ethereal* poked from the jumble of warehouses that clustered around the wharf.

Rat and Roper helped Witch down while Tinker lifted off their bundle of belongings. They were all clean and warmly clad, parting gifts from Henry John Johnson.

"Good-bye," Tinker said. "If you see that old dog again, tell him I'm sorry about the knife. Tell him that."

"Good-bye." Roper shook Columb's hand, then Finn's. "Where's your rope?"

"It's in the bundle. I'll be using it again, but not carrying it. There's no need."

Rat's eyes blinked uncomfortably in the bright sun. "I'll look after Witch," he said. "If you have the time, go out to the abbey and listen for the holy men. They'll be thinking we all deserted them."

"We will, Rat. You were a good friend. God save you kindly."

And then Witch, tears streaming down her face, kissed and hugged them, each in turn. "Do you remember what I told you once?" she whispered to Columb. "That your love of Holy Ireland was greater than even you knew. But that you'd know someday, with the sacrifice? Do you mind that?"

Columb nodded. He didn't trust his voice to speak.

"I was right, wasn't I? It's greater than anything, your love of Ireland?"

Columb nodded again. His throat felt raw and hot.

Witch smiled. "That'll never change. But you'll change. There's room in your heart for more than Ireland. I know, for I'm a witch." She pushed something small and bulky into his hand.

"Good-bye, Finn. Learn a lot from those books, and teach a lot too."

Finn hugged her tight. "There'll be 'Cead mile failte' for you when you come back," he said. "A hundred thousand welcomes."

Then Witch bent and gathered Skibbereen close. "You'll be talking again soon, darlin'," she whispered. "Remember Witch. Say a prayer for her, way over in America, if you've a mind to." She stood abruptly, untangling herself from Skibbereen's clinging arms. "Come on, boyos, let's go."

Columb and Finn and Skibbereen watched till the four figures reached the corner of the wharf. Then Witch turned and shouted something that was carried away and lost in the wind.

"What did she say?" Columb asked anxiously.

Finn smiled. "You didn't hear?"

Columb shook his head.

"She shouted, 'Wait for me, Com. I'll be back before you know it.'"

Columb opened his tightly clenched hands. In them, rolled in a bundle, was the old tweed duncher cap.